ONLY
fools
*
JUMP
*

a novel by

K.P. Haigh

Cover design by DCP Designs

Developmental editing by Judy, Write Techniques

Copyediting by Editing by C Marie

Proofreading by Wendy, The Passionate Proofreader

ISBN: 978-0-9977895-0-8

For my sister, Dawn.

Thanks for letting me steal your romance novels.

Only Fools Jump

Chapter 1

Zoey

I'm jolted awake by a Disney brigade marching right beside my ears, complete with what I swear are symbols, a big bass drum, and two very high and slightly off-pitch singers.

My subconscious is just starting to slide down from the driver's seat after a deep sleep, and all I can think is *I don't know how I got here.*

I very carefully crack one eye open to let just enough light in to make out a tiny mop of blonde curls bouncing up and down. *Oh yeah, I remember how I got here.* Too many beers and one failed attempt at safe sex later, there are two identical jumping results of what should have been a very forgettable night.

I'm a walking, talking addition to the cast of MTV's *Teen Mom*, except I am not nearly dramatic enough for a television crew to follow me around all day. The most exciting thing that's happened to me in the last four years is acquiring a moving box full of Disney VHS tapes and DVDs for twenty dollars at a garage sale. Best money I've ever spent.

Granted, I nearly missed the teenage mom cutoff. I was

3

nineteen when I pushed these two monkeys out of that unreasonably small opening in my southern hemisphere.

The singing stops abruptly. "Do you think she's dead?" a tiny voice asks in what should be a whisper but comes out more like a muffled shout.

"Nah, she's just really, really tired," another voice answers.

"Maybe we should tickle her to make sure?"

My eyes shoot open and I jump up, reaching for the first tiny body I can grab. I pull Phoebe in and smack my lips up and down her arms and legs with a dramatic flare while little giggles and shrieks fill the room. I wish I could just breathe them in forever—their sweet aroma of wax crayons and Cheerios. It would be nauseating if it wasn't so goddamn cute.

"Girls! Breakfast!" a voice calls from down the hall.

The chaos subsides for a moment. Phoebe gives me a kiss on the cheek and hops down off the bed, grabbing her sister's hand before they gallop down the hall in unison.

I glance over at the Mickey Mouse alarm clock my dad bought me for my eighth birthday. It was the first birthday after he left my mom, and at the time, I was beyond aggravated that he got me such a lame gift. It wasn't nearly cool enough for my budding pre-teen years. I'm pretty sure I just rolled my eyes and muttered the required appreciation. I know I didn't even look up before moving on to the next gift.

It was the last birthday he spent with me before he married Sheila, his dental hygienist, and moved across the country to Oregon. Now, every year I get a card with a perfectly rounded signature: *Michael and Sheila.* He doesn't even care enough to sign the thing himself.

The clock was lame at the time, but I needed an alarm clock. My mom refused to buy me a replacement, so I stuck it on the bookshelf next to my bed between my Harry Potter novels and my jewelry box. Function won out over form.

Story of my life.

"Zoey, you're going to be late!" My mom's right. It's almost 7:00am; I need to get moving.

I slip into some cuffed jean shorts and a t-shirt and grab my messenger bag from the corner by my desk. There are dishes clanking in the kitchen and more giggling. I walk out to see Phoebe with a pot on her head like Davy Crockett and Louisa chasing her around with a wooden spoon.

I would gladly pay out what little savings I have to get that kind of energy, but it looks like I'm stuck with semi-burnt coffee and an energy bar.

My mom turns around from the stovetop where she's finishing scrambling eggs for the girls.

"Morning, Zoey," she says sweetly. She still looks exactly the same as when she cooked eggs for me as a kid: same out-of-the-box dark curly hair that just barely sweeps her shoulders, same flowery apron that would fit right into a 1950s advertisement.

I remember being so nervous to tell her I was pregnant. I felt like I had let her down, the one parent who had stuck beside me, the parent who had packed my lunches and stayed up late to help me glue fake moss down for my Babylon piece of the Seven

World Wonders project in the eighth grade. All that time and effort put into encouraging hard work in school was shot to hell by two blue lines.

I could never have predicted the strong grasp of her hug or the tears that ran down to meet the corners of her upturned lips.

"Life happens," she said. She would be disappointed if I failed a class because I didn't study, or if I didn't go to college because I didn't bother to apply.

But getting pregnant? No, that's just an accidental blessing that makes life a little bit more logistically complicated.

Lucky for me, she was two years away from retiring when I came out of the bathroom after peeing on my sixth stick.

I was on my summer break after graduating from high school. So, instead of moving away to go to a state school by the beach, I stayed home and took courses at a local college while I turned into a beached whale. I've powered through online classes every semester since then.

I am one term of summer projects and a final capstone project away from graduating. It's taken me—oh—about eight hundred bajillion hours, but I can see the finish line ahead. I just need to push through these last few months, and then I'm on to a big-kid job in graphic design. I have a mini dance party every time I think about it. I'm going to finish my degree in graphic design and have a job doing the thing that takes my doodles from the corners of the margins to full page, every page.

The degree isn't paying for itself quite yet though, which is why I'm grabbing the keys to my 1993 little-blue-Volvo-that-could and my hoodie before dashing out the door.

"Bye, Mommy!" Phoebe and Louisa chime together as I kiss them on the foreheads.

"Bye Mom, bye girls. I'll be back for bedtime," I cry out.

I stuff the key into the ignition of Sir Chugs-A-Lot and bite into the oddly gritty peanut butter energy bar. I had to take this job when it fell into my lap. I don't get any more free passes in life. I am a single mom of two little girls. My choices are: work my ass off, or work my ass off. I might as well work toward something I love while doing something I have a twin-sized bucket of experience in.

Chapter 2

Zoey

Nineteen-and-a-half minutes later, I pull into the driveway of a four-thousand-square-foot Spanish-style mansion in one of the nicest neighborhoods in Chapel Hill.

In high school, everyone wanted to score a babysitting gig in this neighborhood. The mommy network is tightknit: if you impress one, you're on speed dial for them all—not to mention the going rate is at least double minimum wage.

A few years ago, a friend of mine from the dance team was one of those lucky few, and she passed my name along after she graduated and moved to New York for school. I got a call from Samantha, a recently divorced corporate lawyer who had a screaming baby and a last-minute weekend business meeting in thirty minutes. I desperately needed some new non-maternity jeans and my girls were already asleep, so my mom took over baby monitor duties and I made it over in under seventeen minutes—my all-time and slightly illegal record.

Samantha's nanny had quit earlier that day. I was obviously a last-minute and somewhat unwelcome replacement, but I knew as Samantha eyed my well-loved yoga pants and unicorn t-shirt, I was her only option.

She returned two hours later to a peacefully sleeping baby and not even a speck of dust in the place.

"I haven't come home to a quiet house since before Stewart was born," she said, eyeing every last surface for something, anything that would explain how I managed it. "Did you give him medicine? I expressly stated in the guidelines I left for you that you were not to give him medicine unless he had a fever of above 100.3."

"Nope, no fever. He's working on some top teeth so I froze a wet washcloth and he seemed to really like that. We had story time and I gave him a warm bath, then he calmed right down and fell asleep in my arms."

"Oh." She was stunned but not unhappy. I didn't realize until later that was as close to a compliment as she gets.

I certainly wasn't going to mention that I had two daughters who had started teething at four months and therefore had plenty of experience in the matter. Something told me being a young mom wasn't going to win me any points.

I was supposed to be a temporary fix for a last-minute situation. Instead, I turned into Stewart's new favorite person, and two years later, I'm the nanny of a small child only a year younger than my own twin daughters.

I've barely clicked the mechanism on the lock fully to the right when I hear the tap-tap-tap of feet racing down the hallway toward the front entrance. I open the door and kneel down with a big grin on my face.

"ZOEY!" Stewart shouts excitedly at the top of his lungs.

"Stewart, what have I said about inside voices?" Samantha asks sternly as she follows him down the hall, a thermos of coffee in one hand and a briefcase in the other. She's wearing a slim-fitting navy pantsuit, her deep auburn hair is pulled back into a perfectly wrapped twist, and even though I know she's wearing some of that absurdly expensive makeup she has neatly lined up in her immaculate master bath, you'd never know it. She is the picture they post under the definition of corporate lawyer. She's a walking, talking stock photo.

We are nothing alike at all.

My blonde waves are haphazardly knotted on the top of my head and there is a fifty percent chance this shirt came from the dirty pile on my floor and not the clean-but-I'm-too-lazy-to-actually-put-it-away pile. There is most definitely a ketchup stain on the bottom right, but it's faded enough to not necessarily give any insight into the clean/dirty debate.

But, we both love the slightly blond, perfectly squishy little boy I've pulled up onto my hip.

"Thank you for being on time," she snaps out like a tyrannical alligator. "I have a very full day, and I can't waste a minute in traffic. Everything is status quo; I will see you at 6:00pm."

"Thanks, Samantha! Have a great day!" I say brightly. Her curt demeanor took some getting used to, but she's never late. She pays me on time, and I always get an extra check for my birthday and Christmas. I can't fault her for not having a warm and fuzzy personality. She doesn't walk all over me, which is more than I can say for other nannies I've talked to whose bosses take advantage of them—running late and expecting extra time on top of normal weekday duties without a single extra cent.

It helps that Samantha hasn't been on a date the entire time I've known her. If she needs me for an extra nighttime event, it's a work function, and it's almost always planned weeks in advance.

I always get to go home to see my girls, and Samantha can stay blissfully unaware of the fact that she hired a girl who got pregnant in high school as the nanny for her son—a fact I'm sure would result in my immediate termination. To her, I'm a poor girl in her early twenties, working her way through college at turtle speed. That's forgivable, potentially admirable even. Being able to qualify as a member of the *Teen Mom* cast? Not so much.

I wait for the sound of the door to the garage swinging shut with a soft thud. Stewart knows the cue as well as I do; he practically leaps out of my arms, wobbling unsteadily as he lands on his feet.

"What do you want to do today, buddy?"

"I want to build a FORT!" he announces happily, running toward the barely used dining room to grab the absurdly expensive Restoration Hardware chairs and turn them into a pillow and sheet wonderland. I remember that I snagged a string of Christmas lights before they were put away in storage, and I make a mental note to grab those and some mess-free snacks to complete this building experience.

I'm not proficient in many things in life, but I'm a pro at taking care of tiny humans.

Chapter 3

Zoey

Four hours later, every couch in the whole house has been stripped of its cushions and the dining room is a magical fort wonderland. Stewart was so tuckered out, he went down for a nap—a glorious treat these days. He's old enough that he doesn't always want to sleep during the day, even though he shows all the classic sleep-angry signs.

Our destruction is limited to the dining room. I know if I torch our fort creation, he'll be disappointed when he wakes up, and hell, I can get at least another two hours of playtime out of this thing. Don't mess with what works.

I steal a few pillows and turn on the TV in the family room, clicking over to a home design show where they restore old homes that are falling apart. It's a luxury to be able to take a few moments for myself, and it's only for a few days since I start classes again soon. This is the sweet spot where naptime doesn't equal cram-in-as-much-as-homework-as-possible time.

They're just getting to the big reveal when a loud pounding knocks the silence off its hinges. The deliveryman doesn't normally knock, but sometimes Samantha has special couriered documents delivered which I have to sign for. She always lets me know ahead of time and then texts me two seconds after she receives the delivery confirmation email to verify that I got them. It's strange that she didn't mention anything.

The pounding repeats, and I silently curse the person on the other side of the door. *Of course.* Of course they have to make a ton of noise while there's a child sleeping. *If you wake him up, you get to deal with the grumpy toddler-gremlin a half-nap creates,* I promise silently.

As I pull the door open, I see a flash of yellow pulling out of the driveway and the broad back of a man carrying a black leather duffel bag over his shoulder.

"Um, can I help you?" I ask.

He turns around, and I feel a spark ignite at the edge of every tiny hair as they stretch away from my skin, drawn to the gorgeous specimen of a man standing in front of me.

It takes me a minute to recover from my reaction. You can't blame me; it's a lot to take in. His thick, wavy dark hair frames his espresso-swirled eyes, and his crooked smile is currently directing its disarming effect at me, full power.

Which way is up again?

Shut it down, Zoey, the only rational sliver left in my head urges. Just because a cute boy shows up on your doorstep—scratch that, your boss's doorstep, your very *strict* boss—does not mean your lady parts need attention. It's practically the ice age down there, and everyone is better off if it stays that way.

"You must be the nanny," he says.

"Um, yes?" I confirm reluctantly. It's unnerving that this stranger knows more about me than I do about him.

"I'm Elliott." I do a quick mental scan of the Rolodex...nope, nothing. He notices the blank look on my face and adds, "Samantha's brother."

His statement immediately throws me back into the normal rotational pull of Earth. "Um, yeah, that's not possible. Samantha doesn't have a brother."

Elliott's smile falls for a split second, but his poker face is pretty solid. He recovers quickly.

"I hate to break it to you..." Elliott pauses, waiting for my introduction. I let him hang for a moment, but his smile doesn't slip for even a second.

Ugh, I hate awkward pauses. They make my skin crawl and my mind go into overdrive.

Fine, you called my chicken, Elliott. You win this one—whoever the hell you are. "Zoey. I'm Zoey."

"Nice to meet you, Zoey," he says while offering his hand.

I reluctantly grab it, which immediately sends a surge through the threads of my nerves as they explode at every ending.

"Nice to meet you too." I'm so discombobulated I don't even register what I'm saying until I hear it tumble out of my mouth. My southern manners are kicking in. I can't stop my born-and-bred instincts from being utterly polite and welcoming, even if it would make my life easier for Elliott to hop right back into the cab that brought him here.

15

It doesn't help that even in a hoodie and jeans, he looks like he could show up at a J. Crew photo shoot and fit right in. He's rocking laidback casual with a finesse I've never even dreamt of. Ketchup-stained t-shirt is not exactly a look that says *come and get 'em*.

I have to keep it together. Politeness aside, I have no idea who this man is. "I'm sorry, but you're not Samantha's brother."

"Yes, I am."

"No. You're not." I cross my arms and give him my best serious face—perfected over years of dealing with pint-size tantrums.

Elliott stops for a second, wrapping his hand around the back of his neck and squeezing. His eyes start to squint, and I know I'm breaking him down.

He moves his hand up through his hair while he continues to think and somehow, it only ends up more perfectly tousled than before. *Jesus, where did this guy come from? Grey's Anatomy?*

"We can stand out here and argue, or you can show me inside and I can prove to you that Sam and I are actually related."

I squint at him. God, why is it that the first "proof" I think of involves his hands wrapped around my waist? Yeah, not at all relevant to the whole related-or-not-related-to-my-boss issue. *Get it together, Zoey.*

It doesn't help his case that he keeps using a nickname for his sister. Everyone always uses her full name. "There's no way Samantha lets anyone call her Sam."

Elliott's mouth tilts up into a smirk. "Only those who have

enough dirt on her to be able to blackmail her for the rest of the century can."

Damn, his smile should come with a warning label—*caution: may cause complete and utter brain failure.*

I need to sort this out before my brain turns into a complete mushball. "Fine. Let me try to get ahold of her." I pull my phone out of my back pocket, swipe it open, and click my way over to her office number.

The line rings, and I try desperately not to stare at Elliott. It's like trying not to look at a solar eclipse. Everyone tells you you'll go blind, but you still want to sneak a peek anyway.

The ringing stops and a chirpy voice answers, "Hi, this is Melissa, Samantha MacCallister's assistant. How may I help you?"

Melissa? Hmm, must be a new one. I shouldn't be surprised; Samantha makes Miranda Priestly look like an assistant-loving saint. I explain the situation and ask if Samantha's available. She's not. I ask if Melissa knows of said brother. She says she knows Samantha has a brother but she doesn't remember his name. I would roll my eyes, but I highly doubt not knowing a long-lost brother's name ranks high on Melissa's list of problems. I'm about to let her go when she adds that she thinks it starts with an E. Okay, that's somewhat helpful. I thank her and press end.

Hmm. I'm less worried that he's a complete weirdo, but I still wouldn't mind birth certificate-level confirmation here. "Okay, you can come in, but I need proof," I relent, turning around and letting him follow me in.

17

Chapter 4

Zoey

I need a glass of cold water. Colder than cold. Antarctic levels of cold.

As I make my way back to the kitchen, I hear Elliott taking his shoes off—a point in his favor in this whole "related" business. Anyone who knows Samantha knows she's a shoes-off-in-the-house kind of person, and if you think she wouldn't notice, you're dead wrong. I'm pretty sure she has magnifying glasses for eyes. She can see a speck of dust from across the room. Really, it's a miracle Stewart doesn't live in a hermetically sealed bubble.

Argh, what did I come into the kitchen for? I look around the counters until I spot a glass. *Aha! A cold glass of water. Right.* I grab it and fill it with about eight million ice cubes and some water from the tap. That should bring the heat in this situation down, oh, about one tenth of a degree, but hey, you've got to start somewhere.

Elliott walks in with his hands in his pockets. I take a sip of water. Nope, that did nothing to bring down the heat factor.

"Can I get you anything? Water, tea, soda?" I hear myself

asking. Chalk it up to my automatic response system for houseguests. He might murder me with an ice pick in a second, but at least I offered him a beverage.

"I'll have a Gatorade. I'm sure Sam keeps some stashed in there. Thanks." Another point in his favor: Samantha totally does keep Gatorade in the fridge—it's the only non-organic, high-sugar thing in there.

I walk over to the fridge and make the mistake of looking at Elliott on my way over. He's smiling at me, and I notice he has a single dimple on his right cheek. It's like the universe knew giving him two dimples would be unfair to the rest of us.

Ahh. I need to focus. "Okay, so how are you going to prove you're really who you say you are? Do you happen to have a DNA test in your back pocket?"

And what fine pockets they are. His jeans are the perfect cross between hipster slim and boringly straight. He's obviously well-acquainted with the inside of a gym because I can see the outline of his quads through the dark denim all the way from here.

Elliott's eyes lock onto mine when I finally make it back up to his face. His eyebrows tick upward. Yup, I'm pretty sure he realizes I was just checking out his denim—and everything underneath it. I open the fridge door and stick my head in while my cheeks turn hot pink.

"Nope, no DNA test, just my iPhone. You can call my mom if you want. Although, I'm sure you'd question if I preprogrammed the contact listed as Mom to be someone who would just go along with this whole scheme."

19

"Your phone!" I exclaim, nearly knocking him over as I turn around. He must have snuck up on me while I was opening the fridge, which would be totally creepy if it weren't for the fact that my first instinct is to sink my hands into the pockets of his gray hoodie and pull him in until there's not even a millimeter of space between me and his positively rock-solid abs.

Thank goodness I have a glass of water in one hand and a Gatorade in the other, preventing me from letting my ridiculous impulses run wild. *Geez Zoey, keep the urges in check.* It's not like it's the first time I've ever seen a hot guy.

I practically shove the Gatorade into his hands and squeeze past him toward the other side of the kitchen island. I need to put the large slab of marble directly between us.

I down my glass of water, nearly giving myself a brain freeze in the process, and try to pull it together.

Ah, phone. Right. "Don't you have pictures of you and Samantha on your phone?"

He looks stumped for a second before he twists open the Gatorade with a loud pop and takes a swig. He pushes himself up to sit on the counter.

"You've got pictures, right? You know, those things you get when you open up the camera app and go click, click?" *Why, hello there, Sass. Glad you could join us today.*

"Yeah, I haven't seen Sam since I got this new phone." He shrugs.

Well, that's a dead end. You'd think it'd be easier to prove you were related to your own sibling.

20

A loud thud from above breaks through my thoughts. Stewart's up from his nap. "Zoey! I'm awake now! Come and get me!"

Elliott's smile practically pushes his cheeks all the way up to his eyes. At least he has that going for him—he knows about and cares for his nephew. You can't fake that kind of happiness. Elliott pops off the counter and pushes his sleeves up his tanned forearms.

"Can you just stay down here for a second?" I ask kindly. I have no idea how Stewart will react to a new person after waking up, and it's totally possible that it's been years since they've seen each other. He may not even remember his uncle, and we still have the minor issue of proving that major fact.

Elliott almost looks like he's going to open his mouth to disagree, but then he nods and steps back to lean against the counter. I offer a quick "thanks" before running up the back staircase tucked behind the walk-in pantry.

I quickly grab Stewart and pull him up onto the curve of my left hip—those extra midnight bowls of Lucky Charms cereal are actually doing my nanny gig a service by giving me a little extra shelf room.

Stewart tucks his head into the soft dip at the bottom of my neck, and I can smell the sweet scent of his hair. It's my favorite time of day with him. He's always alert but still snuggly as he works on fully waking up from his nap.

I spot the tall mop of brown hair standing next to the mantel as I make my way down the stairs. Stewart lifts his head off my

21

shoulder with happy recognition then jumps out of my arms, charges toward Elliott, and wraps his arms around his leg.

"Uncle Elliott!"

I watch as Elliott dips down and the two grip each other in a bear hug. I look back up at the mantel and realize Elliott was standing in front of a family photo that looks straight out of the nineties, frosted hair tips and all. Even though the boy standing next to Samantha is wearing glasses and neon braces, it's definitely Elliott—one right-sided dimple and all.

"I didn't know you had an uncle, Stewart." It's half comment, half question. Seriously, how did I watch this kid for two years without hearing about an uncle? Although, I guess he's never heard about a certain pair of my family members.

Stewart looks up at me with a grin that's practically as wide as his face. "Mommy tells me stories about him at night, and we talk on the iPad sometimes."

Elliott's eyes twinkle at me like a big fat *I told you so* is just beneath the surface.

I guess my boss really does have a brother—a really absurdly attractive model of a brother who brought a large duffel bag with no heads up. Samantha's going to be pissed.

Well, at least I'm going to get my eight glasses of water a day, because as long as he's around, I'm pretty much guaranteed to be an overheating mess.

Great.

Chapter 5

Elliott

Four hours later, every single toy Stewart has ever owned is scattered somewhere along the floor of his room, the hallway, or the stairs. Even though I'm totally wiped from a day of travel, I will gladly sugar-high myself until bedtime just to hang out with this little dude. I saw him two Christmases ago for a day while I was on a layover to New York, but he's changed into almost an entirely different person in that span of time. They're not lying when they say kids grow up fast.

That's not why I came home, but it certainly doesn't hurt now that I'm here.

Neither does his hot nanny. I don't know what I was expecting—a middle-aged bilingual woman who reminded me more of my fourth grade teacher than the girl on the last Sports Illustrated swimsuit cover? Because Zoey definitely falls into the second category.

I was planning on crashing here under the radar to recover from the damage of the past few months, but now I'm wondering if that's such a good idea.

I'm pretty sure not hooking up with the nanny is rule number two in Sam's book, straight after not getting her house dirty. So, on second thought, if I've already screwed myself on rule number one…

I hear the garage door begin to rumble, and all three of our heads dart to the window overlooking the round circular entrance to the house. There's a flash of silver that pulls in; yup, that's Samantha. Time to face the guillotine.

You'd think being family would mean there's an open door policy in place—especially since she's obviously not lacking space. I know I'm going to eat shit for showing up unannounced, but this isn't the first time I've had to deal with the Kraken.

"Mommy!" Stewart exclaims, jumping up and over a stack of Legos, only managing to step on two or three in the process. I don't know how he does it—stepping on those tiny sharp-cornered devices of torture has got to be one of the levels in hell, but he doesn't even wince as he rounds the corner and rushes toward the stairs.

I smile at Zoey, and she returns my brazen enthusiasm with only a hesitant upturn of her lips. I have the strange urge to protect her, and I have no idea where that's coming from. I brush it off and try to focus on the situation.

I need a place to crash until the dust settles on my departure from San Francisco, and my sister's pool house is the best place to do that.

The garage door opens, and I hear Stewart's high-pitched string of explanations about today's adventures wafting up through the house.

"I'd better go downstairs," Zoey says solemnly, as if she's heading down to face her judge and jury. I nod and follow her to the main staircase that rounds down to the foyer.

Seriously, we wouldn't even be in the same house. How can my sister refuse?

Just as I reach the bottom step, I hear, "Where's my brother?"

I turn the corner of the railing to see Sam carrying Stewart with her lips glued in a flat line and her eyes fierce.

Zoey is ten steps in front of me and from this angle I can see her open her mouth to speak, but I jump in before she even has a chance. "Right here, Sam."

"And why are you right here exactly, Elliott?"

I start to respond, but from the look on Sam's face, it was clearly meant as a rhetorical question. Zoey looks as if she's trying to shrink away into the wall and become invisible. She is stuck dead in between the two of us. This is not a game of monkey in the middle where she wins.

"I got a memo from my assistant that you were at my house. I had to stop everything and cancel the rest of my meetings so I could get home to make sure you weren't harassing my nanny into letting you in. You gave me no warning. No phone call. Not even an email."

I can feel the rage radiating out from her core. She lives by rules. Order. Law. My unexpected arrival violates her principles. *Screw that.* "I'm your baby brother. I'm allowed to show up on your doorstep unannounced. It's part of the older sister gig. It's part of the contract," I say with a laugh.

Sam continues to glare at me, but I'm not letting her lawyer bullying get to me.

"You didn't have to race home," I continue firmly, "and I didn't call because I thought I was going to crash with some friends for a while, but their surfing trip was extended and they're not home. So, I showed up here. I figured you and Stewart would have space for me and that maybe you'd like to spend some family time together."

Bam. There's the family card; it's Sam's weakness. She loves Stewart more than anything else in the world, and we both know it. Her shoulders release and her Kraken starts to dive again, shrinking beneath the surface.

"Fine. How long are we having family time for?" she asks as if she wants to know how long the sewer pipe is going to be backed up. I would be offended if I wasn't her brother; I know Sam isn't exactly the affectionate type.

"Oh, I don't know, a week or two. I need to line up my next gig." I see Zoey shift at my statement. I don't know why, but her eyes go wide for a split second. Having company while she takes care of Stewart is probably not high on her list of goals for the summer.

"Okay, well, you're making dinner," Sam declares before heading upstairs with Stewart still on her hip.

I'll take it. The kitchen of my last place was about the size of a twin bed, and not one of those extra long ones they put in dorm rooms. I'll gladly spend a little time in Sam's obnoxiously souped-up kitchen. I know she has all the best tools even though she probably eats the same microwavable, organic diet shit for dinner every night.

Before I've even made it two steps, Zoey is over to the front door with her bag slung over her shoulder.

"I need to… Um, bye," she says awkwardly, swinging the door open and fleeing outside. I have no idea if she's normally like this or if today threw her off, but damn, I want to stick around and find out.

Too bad I'm going to stay out of her hair. I don't need any more complications in my life.

Chapter 6

Zoey

Elliott doesn't exist for a grand total of five minutes on my drive home—the part where I'm dealing with the idiots who don't know how to merge onto the I-40 out of Chapel Hill. As soon as I take my exit and find myself squarely on the back roads to my house, my focus breaks and I find my mind pulled magnetically back to the completely off-limits boy who just moved into the pool house.

I wonder what he was doing in California. Was his leaving scandalous or just good timing? Is his—*ahem*—girlfriend missing him?

I have no idea if he even has a girlfriend, but what guy looks like that and is still on the market? I mean, he didn't scream total psycho, and even if he's an asshole on wheels, he's attractive enough that some girl somewhere would be idiot enough to put up with it. Hashtag real talk.

Let's be honest, Phoebe and Louisa's dad isn't going to win nice guy of the year. We got it on in the back of his pickup truck —how very southern of us. At the time, I thought it was romantic

—like a scene from a movie that just needed the right soundtrack. In reality, I was just tipsy enough to not notice that it was dirty and cold. Three-and-a-half minutes on your back on freezing, hard plastic does not a fairytale make.

When I told him I was pregnant, he told me I'd have to handle it by myself. He had a scholarship to play at a fancy state school halfway across the country, and being a dad was not part of that plan.

He got points for not questioning if he was the father, but those points have been the only ones in his bucket for a long time. Neither the girls nor I have heard a peep from him since. He was honest, I'll give him that, but it doesn't mean I haven't cursed him six-ways-to-Sunday a time or two.

One thing's for sure: I'm not going to find out if Elliott can break the three-and-a-half minute record. A few things have changed, and one of them is my standards.

Besides the inherent cobwebs of my lackluster sex life, sleeping with my boss's brother is pretty much dating in the workplace, especially when he currently resides at said workplace.

So, while it may feel good in the moment, everyone gets screwed eventually—and not in the good way.

Ugh, why couldn't Samantha's brother have been some rich country club type with a sweater tied over his shoulders and a throwback comb-over? Then I would have no trouble whatsoever not being attracted to him in the slightest.

But Elliott? This is going to take effort. We're talking serious willpower—like giving up chocolate AND swearing AND Netflix binges AND wine for Lent. I don't exactly have a great Lent track record. I think the last time I gave something up was in the third grade when Jessica Swartzmore convinced me the Easter Bunny wouldn't come unless I gave up something for Lent. I should have known something was up when she suggested I give up the Twinkie my mom packed in my lunchbox every day. Even then, I only lasted two weeks of Jessica gladly benefiting before I gave up.

A week or two, I remind myself. That's what he said. I can handle that. A dozen days, give or take. They'll fly by, and I don't stick around on weekends. Elliott will probably be gone during the weekdays, interviewing or whatever it is normal twenty-somethings do during the day.

I'll probably see him for an hour or two a day max, and I'll be focused on Stewart.

Yes. A few hours total. I can handle being around the most attractive man I've ever met for that amount of time. It's the time it takes to play Monopoly, and I'm sure it will be just as boring. I'll collect my paycheck, pass go, and all will be well.

This will be easy-peasy. It'll almost be like he doesn't even exist.

The image of him diving into the pool butt naked flashes through my head. *Damn, I bet he has a butt that's worth getting caught staring at.* I let out a frustrated moan. This is not helping.

I pull into the driveway of our house and park. At least I have something to distract me at home—two very entertaining, highly energized somethings I can't wait to see.

I've barely made it through the door when Phoebe and Louisa

barrel at me like wild pigs—adorable, tiny teacup pigs, but still.

"Guess what, Mom?" Louisa chirps.

Before I can respond, Phoebe—who is never one to wait for the punch line—shouts, "Aunt Cassie is coming home!"

I didn't know Cassie was coming home from her third year at UCLA, but we haven't exactly been able to catch up with long phone chats about our personal lives. Between the girls, nannying, and the three-hour time difference, we only get sporadic text messages. Links to videos of Kristen Bell and Dax Shepard's latest adorableness (from me) and selfies asking about outfit choices (from her, obviously) don't exactly touch on the intricate details of life.

I look back at my mom and she lifts her shoulder with a tip of her head. Apparently, neither one of us knows why our little LA actress is venturing back home. Whatever the reason is, I can relate to my daughters' enthusiasm. I love my little sister more than Oreos and coffee, and I really, really love Oreos and coffee. *Dude, do they make coffee-flavored Oreos? Because they should.*

"I think we should have a dance party to celebrate," Phoebe says to no one in particular. She would celebrate the sun coming up in the morning with the music turned up, jumping around the living room if she could.

I bend down, putting my palms on each of her soft cheeks, and give her a kiss on the nose.

"Absolutely." I reach over and do the same for Louisa, who looks at me like she has her favorite things in the whole world right in front of her.

31

My shoulders finally start to melt away from my ears, and I let the girls lead me into the living room, pressing play on the dance party playlist on my phone.

Elliott? Who's Elliott?

Chapter 7

Zoey

As I walk up to the bright red door on Monday, I dig into my cross-body bag and listen for the jangle of keys. My fingers slip between old receipts and the stupid mess of tissues that always fall out of those silly little travel packages that won't stay shut.

Monday mornings are the worst. I hate leaving Phoebe and Louisa after having uninterrupted weekend time with them. Even when we're at our worst—when it's one big mess of tantrums and pouting and overblown emotion—I still miss them when I walk out that door.

Sometimes, it's a parental paradox. Life is hard with them and hard without them. I can be beyond thankful to be climbing into my car, escaping with my sanity barely hanging by a thread because these two tiny humans are so much like me. They know exactly how to angle their little fingers so that when they push my buttons it feels like every cell in my body is going to explode.

And yet, I miss them. I miss the high-pitched giggles that tumble out of them so effortlessly. I miss the way they love each other fiercely and also aggravate each other immensely. And

33

somehow through it all, I stand firmly in the center of their wildly brilliant orbits and get to take it all in.

Then, there's my precocious little Stewart. He's not really mine, but he does make the sting of leaving my own two girls a little less painful. I wish I could introduce them. My wild twins would probably have him jumping off furniture in no time, and maybe he would show them how to sit still for more than two seconds.

My two worlds have to stay firmly planted in their own corners. This isn't a Venn diagram; there's no happy overlap.

My fingers finally snag the loop of my keychain and I pull it out toward the door handle as the heavy door suddenly swings open.

I leap back in surprise, like I touched a live wire. It takes my brain a second to process the man standing in front of me in a t-shirt and running shorts. His mouth flicks up to the right in a crooked smile.

"Oh! Elliott! Um, hi!"

God, you'd think I'd be able to form complete sentences around this man, but my brain is just not equipped to handle him. I might not have a bachelor's degree yet, but I most definitely passed the fourth grade. I should be able to form complete sentences with coherent ideas that connect together, but when I'm around Elliott, I'm an incoherent mess. *Come on hormones, take a chill pill already.*

"Hey Zoey, I heard your car pull in and thought it was my buddy coming to pick me up for a few rounds of basketball," he explains. His eyes are glued to mine, and I almost wonder if I send his world a little off kilter too. I push the thought away as quickly as it arrives.

Elliott quickly regains his smile and steps aside. "Come on in," he offers easily. At least one of us knows how to act cool.

When I walk in, I accidentally brush a sliver of his skin and feel a jolt of excitement. Now I really have touched a live wire. I could have sworn I had enough room to pass him; did he take a step toward me?

"Sorry I scared you opening the door," he says with a teasing smile. I don't believe him for a second. I get the sense that he likes seeing me turn into an incoherent mess. *Jerk.*

"Is Samantha here?" I ask, fumbling for something to say. I don't know why I'm asking; of course she's still here. The keys to her very expensive BMW 5 series are still sitting in their spot on the side entry table by her briefcase.

My brain is falling back to the polite small-talk basics—which, hey, I can't complain about, because it sure is a lot better than shouting out *Damn, you look good in gym shorts.* If I ran with that train of thought, I'd probably follow it up with a question about if he works out with or without his shirt on, which might lead to something even worse, like *Is watching you work out a spectator sport?*

Nope. I'll take banal small talk. Much safer. Much less embarrassing.

"Yeah, she's getting ready. Stewart's grabbing his crayons. He said something about design school...?" Elliott looks intrigued but slightly confused.

"Mmm, right. I promised I would help him"—I pause to add air quotes—"*take his art to the next level*. His words, not mine." It makes me smile. I'm proud that I've contributed to such a curious little boy. He wants to understand what I'm studying, and not just what it is, but how to do it. He made me promise last Friday that I would give him a lesson.

Elliott's eyes crinkle and he lets out a hearty laugh. "He really is my sister's kid sometimes, you know."

All I can think about is how the hell to piece together an even remotely witty response just so I can hear him laugh again. It's such a deep, warm sound, like someone is wrapping you up in a warm hug that smells like cinnamon and sugar. Yet, my brain is not firing on all of its witty cylinders. Hell, it hasn't been since I gave birth. Motherhood is kind of like drinking: everything gets a little hazy and you knock out a few thousand brain cells in the process.

Thankfully, Elliott leads us into the expansive white and marble kitchen and opens the fridge. "Can I get you anything?" he offers politely, the tables oddly turned from yesterday. Now I feel like the stranger in this house and he's the welcoming southern host.

Is it weird that I kind of wish he was an asshole? Because this whole extraordinarily good-looking AND polite shtick is not helping matters. It's hard not to be attracted to someone when they're offering you a beverage with a smile that could launch a thousand Crest white-strips commercials.

I wrinkle my nose. "No, thanks."

Elliott shrugs, pulls out a Gatorade, and sits down on a stool at the island. I lean against the far edge of the kitchen countertop. Distance is my friend here—so is a quick exit.

"So, you've been Stewart's nanny for a while?"

"Yeah, a couple years." I don't stop to think before I continue, "I'm kind of surprised I haven't seen you before." The statement just slips out. I mean, it is a little odd I never knew he existed.

Elliott stares at me for a long breath, and I can't tell if he's angry that I'm unintentionally calling him out for not being around or just really focused on how to respond. His eyes are narrowed in on my face, and his lips are as flat and straight as the blade edge of one of Samantha's absurdly expensive knives.

Maybe I've pissed him off, which is probably a good thing. If he hates me, then he'll go out of his way to avoid me and the rest of this summer will be washboard ab-free.

"I was busy," he finally responds, tugging on the lobe of his ear. His eyes soften and the straight line of his mouth curves ever so slightly down. "I was too busy. I made a lot of bad decisions the past few years."

I can feel the weight he's carrying around in his words; it mirrors the heaviness of the coulda-woulda-shoulda brigade I've been carrying around. I became a mom at nineteen, but I have no idea what has kept Elliott away for the last few years.

I feel a magnetic pull toward him, a desire to pull open the shutters on his thoughts and throw light onto every surface. It's everything I can do to hold tightly to this counter at the opposite

37

end of the room. One step closer and I risk being pulled in and becoming too intrigued to be able to step away.

I have to keep my distance.

I want to know more, but I cut that desire off before it gets any further.

"Mm, well, I'm sure Samantha and Stewart are happy to have you here now." Elliott looks almost disappointed by my response. His eyes close for a second longer than a blink. When they open, I add in a smile for good measure. I have to be distant, but it doesn't mean I have to be a dick.

Then, in another blink, it's back to the Elliott I keep running into at the door: charming Elliott with an easy smile. He takes a sip from his drink and smirks. "I don't know that Sam's exactly happy I'm crashing in the pool house, but she's stuck with me."

It's a good thing I didn't take him up on his offer to drink because I'm pretty sure I'd either be choking or spewing said liquid everywhere to keep from saying that I'm pretty sure no one in the history of ever would consider his presence something they're *stuck* with.

Saying things like that would not keep me on neutral ground here, and I desperately need to stay on neutral ground. I'm standing at border control for Switzerland, begging them to let me in.

Thank god I hear Samantha making her way downstairs and the hum of an engine pulling into the driveway.

"That doesn't look like interview attire, Elliott," Samantha clucks from behind me.

"Nah, I was going to grab some coffee, work through my emails for a bit, and then play basketball with some buddies from high school." He grins brazenly. "Good networking," he adds as he heads out of the kitchen, back to the front door. I glance back at Samantha and see only the tiniest flicker of an eyebrow raise. I don't know that I've ever seen someone so unfazed by her. The gardener practically has heart palpitations every time he sets foot in the yard.

The only one who is the least bit flustered here is me, and I learned long ago that Samantha is more bark than bite—at least in my case. She needs someone to take care of her child and replacing me would take too much time and effort, otherwise my temporary babysitting gig turned full-on nanny job would never have happened.

No, my inability to take more than quick, shallow breaths is attributed to the other MacCallister in the room.

It's no wonder Switzerland is holding me at arm's length.

Before I can even consume one full, satisfying sip of oxygen, Stewart is in front of me with his crayons ready and both of the MacCallister siblings are out the door.

I haven't taken a step away from the kitchen counter yet, and I feel like the slightest movement will annihilate my already shaky equilibrium.

I am in so much trouble.

Chapter 8

Elliott

I can't even think—that's how tired my muscles are. They've interrupted all regularly scheduled programming with tiny screams of pain. *Jesus, when did I get out of shape?* It's not like I didn't work out when I was in Cali—it was the total opposite actually. Everything is about fads out there. The current favorite was a routine of twenty minutes every single day of hardcore weight training. So, I hit the gym every day. Short, painful, done.

Apparently, playing a pickup game of basketball is not on the roadmap of achievements in the twenty-minutes-a-day plan.

I sit down on the bench that runs the length of the court and grab the water out of my bag. Most of the guys have left already, heading back to their jobs after filling their lunch break with basketball. My buddy Brandon finishes saying goodbye to the last couple guys and walks over.

"Good game," he says between laughs, the corner of his mouth lifted.

"You kicked my ass and you know it." I'm exhausted, but it feels good. Brandon nods in agreement and grabs his water, taking a seat.

"It's good to have you back." Brandon doesn't look over when he says it, but I don't have to see his face to believe him. I've known Brandon since we were in grade school, and he's not the type to go all sentimental.

I get it though—there's something about history that makes it impossible to replace the friends you grew up with. It's part of the reason I never really felt like Cali was home. I could hang out with people all day and night, but it just wasn't the same.

"Good to be back." This part is true. The circumstances that led to my departure…not so much.

I moved out to San Francisco with every intention of becoming worthy of all those thirty-under-thirty lists. There was a substantial amount of ego involved there, I know that, but when you're raised by a man who thinks he's God's gift to law, a little bit of over-inflation is expected.

I started a company and grew it into something I was proud of, but money dried up. Everything went from buzzing to silent in a matter of weeks.

I had to lay off twelve people—people who had families, rent payments, college loans. I'd put everything I had into that company. Every decision, personal and professional, was made to keep it going. I wasn't alone. Most of my coworkers skipped birthday parties, vacations, time with friends. We believed in what we were doing.

Right up until we weren't doing it any more.

I didn't make Stewart a priority for two years, and what do I have to show for it? An empty bank account and a list of people who depended on me, on my judgment, who got screwed.

Someday, I'll say it was humbling. Today, I say it was just fucking brutal. No one should have to call in their colleagues— their friends—and tell them there's barely enough for severance. Some of them found jobs, but a lot of them are still looking.

I know I didn't cause it, but I was steering the ship and accidentally scraped an iceberg. It came out of nowhere, and I didn't move quickly enough to avoid it. It's not my fault, but it doesn't mean I was an innocent bystander of the ship now at the bottom of the ocean.

I would have stayed in California and drunk my sorry ass off, but it was too damn expensive.

"How long you sticking around for?" Brandon asks as he scrolls through emails on his phone. As the son of a pharmaceutical mogul, he could have coasted for most of his life. Instead, he learned the business and works as an analyst in the same company his dad practically built with his research.

I shake my head. I have no fucking clue. There's no way I'm heading back out west, but just because I know what I don't want doesn't mean I have any clue about what I do want. I'm not even ready to think about that yet.

"Well, I'm going to keep dragging you out to shoot hoops with us. You're fun-employed. No excuses."

"I appreciate it." It's not a bad idea to get out of the house and get my ass kicked twice a week…and avoid Zoey.

Logic tells me I should stay away, but I find myself thinking about her anyway. There's something about her that intrigues me. Maybe it's the way she interacts with Stewart like he's the highlight of her day rather than something to keep an eye on while she scrolls through Instagram updates.

Maybe it's the fact that she's managed to deal with my sister for two years, which means she must be made of iron underneath that ridiculously smooth skin of hers. The way her ass curves underneath those shorts doesn't hurt either.

It doesn't matter, because it's not a good idea. I'm not the kind of guy she needs to get involved with, and our situation is way too complicated to even fantasize about.

"And let me know when you're ready to talk business; I've got a few ideas I want to run by you." Brandon's voice stops my train of thought and throws a new one onto the tracks. We used to joke about starting our own companies when we were kids. In our high school yearbook, he was named most likely to be the CEO of a Fortune 500 company. He has it in him; I don't know if I do any more.

"Sure." I know we'll sit down at some point, have a beer, and talk shop. Just not today…or tomorrow…or maybe even the rest of this summer. I'm not ready to jump back in. Not yet.

Chapter 9

Zoey

By the time we roll into the next week, I think I've found my rhythm.

It basically consists of doing everything in my power to avoid Elliott and sticking to one-word answers when I can't.

He probably thinks I'm a freak, but I've also avoided a) losing my shit and humping him like a puppy on a chair leg and b) consequently losing my job and ending up in a psych ward.

I'll take weirdo over unemployed any day.

It helps that Elliott has mostly been MIA. I guess that's what it means to have an active social life. Ha, I've forgotten what that looks like. Between school, the girls, and Stewart, my calendar doesn't really leave room for much else.

It's all going to flip when my classes finish at the end of this term. I'll still have my final project, but I won't have to go to campus every week. In September, Stewart goes into full-day Montessori preschool, so he won't need a full-time nanny any more, which means I need to find a job—or at least an internship—in the field I've actually been studying. You know, not the diaper-changing, tantrum-settling career path I've become a three-time expert in.

I love Stewart, but this was never meant to be a permanent gig. I've been lucky it's lasted this long, but man, I need to join the adult world where I can have real conversations about… Wait, what do adults actually talk about? I have no stinking clue.

Oh well. Step one, figure out relevant grownup interests. Step two, discuss.

I realize I've been staring at the piece of blank paper in front of me with a colored pencil in my hand without blinking for god knows how long. I think my eyeballs have started to dry out and shrivel up. I push the sharp edge of blue to the white sheet with a satisfying glide. I haven't decided what I'm going to draw yet, but sometimes you just have to start with a line before you figure out where to go next.

I look up at Stewart; he has been sitting quietly, coloring a myriad of family portraits, including a dog he doesn't have and a blue elephant standing next to stick figures that look like him and his mom. I really hope I'm not the elephant. I'm not even going to ask.

I started out showing him how to draw some of the famous brand logos and how to play around with turning shapes into bigger objects—like using triangles and circles to draw people. When I asked him what he wanted to draw, he said he wanted to put what he saw in his head on paper. I've spent years trying to learn how to do that, and yet he does it without even thinking about it. How are kids so brilliant without even realizing it?

It's getting close to naptime, so I need to get some of his energy out if I have any hope of him going down for a snooze.

"Stewart, we've been inside for a while today. Want to go outside and play?"

It's hard to get outside in the summer here. The heat lands on your skin and sinks in so quickly you barely have a minute before it feels like your insides are melting. It's worth it though if we run around for a while and he gets tired enough to want to nap. The more I can wear him out, the better life will be.

He doesn't look up but keeps working intently on the elephant's crown made out of lightsabers—at least that's what it looks like. No matter how long I spend around kids, I'll never be able to figure out what's going through their heads.

"Come on," I nudge gently. "We can play tag?" I get a shrug. "Or kick around the soccer ball?" Nothing. "What about going for a swim?"

Stewart finally looks up from his drawing, his pencil held perfectly still in his hand. *Aha, gotcha, kid.*

"Do I have to put on sunscreen?" he asks. Yeah, Stewart's obviously the offspring of a lawyer; he's a pro at bartering.

"Yes, but I have some of the spray-on kind your mom hates in my bag. We can use that if you want."

Samantha refuses to use anything but the zinc oxide stuff, but it takes forty-five-and-a-half years to rub the thick paste in. Stewart is the most chill kid I've ever met, and even he hates it. I started stashing a bottle of the good kind in my bag because hey, it gets him outside AND he doesn't get a sunburn. The zinc oxide can take a back seat to accomplishing the first two objectives.

Case in point, Stewart jumps up and makes a mad dash for the stairs up to his room. Five minutes later, we're downstairs ready to go, which, with a three-year-old, is practically impossible without witchcraft. They should just call me Zoey Porter, Toddler Sorceress Extraordinaire. Yup, that's going to get me all the jobs.

I pack up our coloring tools while Stewart drinks a glass of water. I try not to think about any of the ten things that are my own personal blue elephants dancing around my head. Elliott. Getting a job in graphic design. Elliott. Starting classes again. Elliott. Paying off the rest of my student loans and starting preschool tuition because, surprise surprise, it's not free. Elliott.

I wish I could go back to the days of carefree coloring and playing in the pool and letting grownups handle all the stupid adult bullshit.

"Okay! I'm ready," Stewart cries out happily as he sets down his empty glass and races toward the door. I quickly follow him, pushing those thoughts out of my head.

I am a nanny and a mother. I have to put blinders on and focus. My life is about taking care of tiny humans, not getting lost in a sea of woe-is-me. Swimsuit, sunscreen, and then pool. There isn't room for elephants in that equation. I push them out and follow Stewart outside.

Chapter 10

Elliott

When I open the side door to the mud room, I don't hear anything, and I slowly let out the breath I was unintentionally holding in.

Maybe Zoey took Stewart for a walk to the park or something.

Thank god. I have been doing my damned best to avoid her and her mind-blowing legs all week. She had to have caught me staring because whenever I've seen her, she's barely said more than two words to me. She must think I'm the ultimate loser creep—moving into his sister's pool house. I don't want to make that a loser creep who pops a boner every time I'm around her.

It's been a get-in, get-out situation with the main house. I reach into the fridge for a Gatorade and a few packages of string cheese then make my way back toward the pool. I got my ass handed to me on the court again today and wouldn't mind some time in the water to take the edge off.

I hear Stewart's tiny little giggle with fits of snorting thrown in. I know I should turn around. Pools mean swimsuits, and these gym shorts aren't going to hide a damn thing if I see Zoey.

Something tells me she's not a one-piece kind of girl.

My legs start walking toward the double French doors before my brain can even tell them to stop. Restraint be damned.

As I pull down on the door handle, Stewart catches sight of me, his face lighting up with pure joy. *Shit.* The circumstances that brought me home were less than stellar, but I'd deal with it all over again to get time with my nephew. He doesn't care what happened in San Francisco. He only cares that we have all day Saturday to build the biggest fort anyone has ever seen. I'm his hero, and I haven't done a goddamned thing to deserve it. It's both incredible and humbling. I may not have been around when he was born, but I sure as hell can't stay away now that I'm back.

It only takes Zoey a second to register Stewart's shift in attention. She's quick. She doesn't just sit off on the sidelines, texting the whole world, only glancing up to watch Stewart once every five minutes. I haven't seen her phone out once. She's down on his level playing with him every second.

God, she'd be an amazing mom.

Okay, somebody slap me. I've been around this woman for less than two weeks. I cannot be a walking cheese factory, even if she looks at me like…

Yeah, okay. She's looking at me like *Oh god, why are you here.* It's as if my presence causes her physical pain. Crisis averted, that is exactly the slap I needed. I swing open the door and blast her a megawatt smile.

What? Just because my presence seems to be worse than

Freddy Kruger showing up on Friday the 13th doesn't mean I can't at least try to win her over.

I ask her how her day is going like the good southern gentleman my mom tried but barely succeeded to raise when Stewart pops out of the pool. "Zoey! Look what Uncle Elliott taught me!"

Stewart toddles back to the far edge of the cement surrounding the pool and then makes a mad dash for the water, but as he reaches the section of tile that lines the perimeter, his feet hit the puddle of water he left when he was standing there dripping.

Life slows to the point where I can see each second like a frame in a slow motion projection. Stewart's feet fly up and his momentum drags him forward and down. The great big smile on his face shifts from a half circle to a completely symmetrical ring of surprise.

There is enough energy pulling Stewart forward that when his body catches the rim of the pool, he smacks the edge with a heavy thwack. My whole body clenches at the noise. I'm pretty sure it's the back of his shoulder that takes the brunt of the hit. I quickly thank every single ion in the universe it wasn't half a foot higher. Somehow, Stewart bounces off the pool edge and lands squarely in the water.

I drop my Gatorade before I even think about it and make my own mad dash into the water, jumping in and pulling Stewart out. I know he's not at risk of drowning—Zoey made him wear the arm floats he was complaining about being too old for this past weekend—but the logical part of my brain is being overridden. All I can think of is that he's hurt. He's hurt, and I have to do everything in my power to help him.

Chapter 11

Zoey

I've never seen a human move so fast. It's like The Flash exists in real life, and he's standing right in front of me, soaking wet and holding a very stunned Stewart in his arms.

I give myself a moment to take in the now wet shirt and shorts clinging to every single square inch of his body. I give myself one second to explode into a firework show of lust—a show where they accidentally let off all the fireworks at once in one big, overlapping flash.

One second and then Stewart's shock subsides, my mom brain regains full control of my senses, and those fireworks are dunked with a cold bucket of fix-it mode.

Loud sobs break the slow motion time warp my brain is stuck in and life reverts to standard speed.

I reach out my arms for Stewart but Elliott shakes his head.

"No, I got this," he says as he pulls Stewart upward, cradling Stewart's head against his firm shoulder.

Anger erupts like a fiery follow-up to my earlier fireworks. I'm Stewart's nanny. How dare he tell me he's got this? He's been here less than two weeks and he's already acting like he's a bona fide Stewart expert.

The anger evaporates when I look at Elliott's face. His eyes are pinched together as he feels every one of Stewart's wailing tremors. It doesn't matter who's holding Stewart; we both want to fix him.

I focus on the bright red line that has erupted along Stewart's ribs. I can't tell if he hit a rib or if he somehow managed to catch himself between the two seemingly fragile bones. You'd think our bodies would make the cage that is supposed to protect our vital organs a little more, I don't know, protective?

"How bad is it?" Elliott's voice interrupts my doctoring. Considering my only medical knowledge comes from years of Web MD-ing over my own two daughters, I am not qualified to diagnose this. All the Internet research in the world does not give me a medical license, just a penchant for assuming the worst.

"I don't know!" I snap. Elliott's eyes squint in confusion and then soften, forgiving my angry burst almost immediately.

I wish I knew how bad it was, but I can't tell with the swelling, and Stewart's cries could shatter glass. I wonder if we should ice it, but I doubt that would be a successful exercise. You try icing anything on a toddler for more than two seconds. I worry it could be broken ribs, and I don't want to chance it.

"I think we need to take him to the ER," I say. Elliott just nods his head as he strokes Stewart's hair, trying to keep his body as still as possible.

Elliott asks me to grab a fresh shirt from his suitcase in the pool house while he wrangles Stewart into the car seat in my car. I am in and out in two seconds then race through the house to grab my bag and flip flops before dashing out to the car.

Somehow, Stewart is already in his seat, and his sobs have mellowed into a slower cadence. I don't know how Elliott did it— black magic? He must have sensed my confusion. He mouths, "Ice pack," and points at Stewart's back in the car seat.

Smart.

Elliott doesn't take his eyes off me. I see the ridge of his throat move up slowly and then back down. "Aren't you going to put some clothes on first?"

I glance down, seeing only my hot pink halter two-piece. I quickly thank my past self for putting an extra set of my own clothes in my bag. I mumble something about how I was getting to that part, knowing full well I would have driven all the way to the doctor's office in my bikini and looked like a nanny newbie. I toss Elliott's shirt over the top of the car and unzip my bag, pulling out a spare pair of track shorts and a Rainbow Bright t-shirt. I toss them on over my still half-wet swimsuit. *Good enough.*

When I look back over at Elliott, his shirt is on and his arms are pressed against the top of the car, his eyes transfixed on me. If I didn't know better, I'd say it was the same look he gave me when he opened the door and saw me out at the pool today.

But I do know better. Elliott has been avoiding me like a ginger avoids the sun. He's not lusting after me, he's probably just shocked that I clearly do not have it all together under pressure.

As if on cue, he asks if he can drive. I send him a look that would make even a superhero back down, but he follows it up with the sound advice that maybe I could call his sister and let her know where we're headed.

Argh. Why does he have to be right? I toss him the keys and we quickly run around the front of the car, trading spots. By the time I've buckled in and pulled out my phone, Elliott has reversed us toward the circular turnabout in front of the house. It feels nice to have someone else pilot a toddler crisis for once, but I push the feeling down with a healthy dose of anger.

I dial Samantha's office and her assistant picks up on the second ring.

"Samantha MacCallister's office, how may I help you?" the assistant offers smoothly. I don't recognize the voice, and then I remember Samantha mentioned something about a new assistant last week, but I don't remember her name.

I don't even think the previous one lasted a month. The list of Samantha's short-lived assistants is long; there's no point in keeping track. I just thank my lucky stars I work with Stewart all day. I may report to Samantha, but I'm dealing with Stewart's requests from nine to five, not hers. I doubt I would live up to her standards under constant inspection. Stewart is appeased if he gets in an extra snack time.

"Hi, I'm Zoey, Stewart's nanny. He fell down and hit his back. We're taking him to the emergency room. Can we talk to Samantha?" I blurt it out as fast as the English language will carry me.

"I'm sorry, Samantha is in a meeting," the assistant replies, unruffled.

"I don't think you understand," I say, my octave starting to rise. "Stewart is hurt. We're taking him to the hospital. I want to talk. To. His. Mother."

My blood pressure is starting to reach an uncharted level.

"She said to take messages for all her calls. She doesn't want to be disturbed." Her voice is cool and unsympathetic.

"Her child is hurt! I think she'd want to be disturbed!" I nearly scream into the phone. Elliott reaches over, placing his steady palm on my thigh. My skin tingles at the touch, but I look over and give him the biggest stink eye I can muster. This is not the time for attraction central. I don't want his calming comfort —more like his set-my-skin-on-fire comfort. I want this assistant to do what I'm asking her to do.

"Ms. MacCallister is not to be disturbed. I will give her a message when she's available. Now, is that all?"

I detect the slightest barb under the smooth tone and my inner mom goes crazy. "No. That is not all. Someday, you're going to have a child and you're going to understand what it's like to have your child get hurt. It's the worst feeling in the entire world, and you're going to understand how big a mistake you made just now. Hell, you're going to wish you had let her know when she fires you in a few hours."

I lift the phone off my cheek, wishing there was a receiver I could slam it down on. I settle for pressing the end button firmly and letting out an exasperated sigh.

We ride along in a sob-punctuated silence for a minute before I reach my hand back behind the seat. "It's going to be okay, buddy."

I can see Elliott smile out of the corner of my eye. I turn to face him, and he must notice my gaze because his smile only widens. "Yeah, we're going to be okay, and that assistant is going to be out of a job by the end of the day."

I let a little kindness flow through the tiny hole Elliott has opened in my clenched chest. He's on my side. I didn't know what it felt like to have someone who doesn't share some percentage of your DNA be so firmly in your court.

"Yeah, she's going to take her place in the Samantha MacCallister assistant graveyard, and I don't feel one single bit bad about that."

"Well, aside from you, my sister tends to hire idiotic soulless drones. She lucked out when she found you." Elliott punches a hole through where the tiny opening was just a moment before. He's on my side here. I finally agree with him…we're going to be okay.

Chapter 12

Elliott

I'm surprised we still haven't heard from Samantha by the time we get back home and put Stewart down for a nap. Granted, I have no idea what it really means to be a lawyer, except that she gets paid buckets of cash to intimidate people and to use complicated, practically unintelligible English to do it.

It helps that we were in and out of the ER in just under two hours. Stewart is, in fact, just bruised. Nothing is wrong, and the takeaway is that kids are resilient. I wish I could borrow some of their Wolverine healing powers. My body has taken a beating from my biweekly basketball games.

Zoey was in beast mode the whole time we were there, asking ten million different questions I wouldn't have thought of and making sure everyone moved along at their most efficient yet thorough pace. She was a master, and it was sexy as hell.

When I asked her if she's had lots of practice with this sort of thing, she stopped and gave me the strangest look, muttering something about being prepared. I guess Sam really does end up scaring all her employees eventually. I thought being a nanny meant playing all day and making sure the kid gets some food. I wouldn't be surprised if my sister had Zoey take a full parenting 101 course just to be ready for outliers.

I could see Zoey's thick exterior slowly crumbling as she carried Stewart upstairs, but instead of accepting any help, she shooed me out of his room, exiling me downstairs. It's not even four o'clock yet and I'm exhausted. I'm glad Stewart is okay, but shit, that whole ordeal put me through the wringer.

The soft creak of sneaking footsteps trails into the kitchen.

"He's asleep?" I ask, and Zoey nods soundlessly, even though there are a handful of walls and a whole stretch of square footage between our voices and Stewart's ears. "You've got the monitor?" Another nod. "Good." I motion for her to follow me, and I once again head out the French doors toward the pool house.

I head straight for the kitchenette and open the fridge, pulling out two bottles of water and handing one over to Zoey.

"Sorry, I know it's not the hard stuff, but I think we could both use a breather right now."

"It's okay." Zoey smirks, tucking a strand of hair behind her ear. How can something so simple be so goddamn sexy? "I've got Two Buck Chuck at home."

"Stewart gets banged up a lot? Do you have to pull him out of bar fights every other Friday?"

Zoey blushes, glancing down at the bottle, fumbling to twist the top open. "Umm, no. Just normal, everyday stress, you know? It's a lot, taking care of a tiny human all day."

I nod even though I have no idea what it's like. I tried to build a company from scratch, and something tells me that doesn't hold a candle to what it takes to be a caregiver.

Zoey still hasn't looked back up, even after opening the water and taking a sip. I seize the opportunity to stare.

You wouldn't know that it's a superhuman standing in front of you. She can't be more than five feet tall and her cutoffs and t-shirt vibe only add to her unassuming demeanor, but I wouldn't put money on a grizzly bear in a fight against this girl. She's observant and quick and incredible under pressure. We had to deal with a whole host of medical professionals today, and she didn't cower to a single one of them. It didn't matter that she was the nanny. The one nurse who tried to tell us we needed to wait for Sam in order to move forward was lucky to leave the room with all of her limbs.

Zoey was a pro, and I couldn't have been more attracted to her if she had walked into this pool house and taken off every single item of clothing she had on.

Although I wouldn't say no to that either.

The day was stressful, but it pushed aside whatever it was that had limited Zoey to one-word responses around me. I liked getting a peek at the Zoey behind the curtain, and it confirmed what I already knew but hadn't entirely admitted yet: I'm attracted to her, and I'm starting to lose my willpower to stay away.

But, she works for my sister, and even though Sam doesn't scare me for a second, I have no doubt she would fire Zoey if we set a single toe over the friendship line. I'm not ready to have another job cut because of me, and it really would be my fault this time.

No, I can't get romantically involved with Zoey, but maybe I can just focus on getting to know her. She won't be Stewart's nanny forever, and in the meantime, there's no harm in learning more about each other.

I look over at her freckle-kissed cheeks and know I'm lying to myself. This isn't a harmless pursuit, but I'm going to toe the line anyway.

Chapter 13

Zoey

Ahhh. What is it about Elliott that trips me up? I've been doing this job for more than two years and I haven't once let it slip that, *oh hey, by the way, I'm a single mom who got pregnant when I was still a teenager.*

I need this gig. I am so close to the end of my degree, and this paycheck is already spoken for. Student loans are no joke and tiny humans are not cheap. I have no idea how long it's going to take for me to find a job in graphic design. This isn't the beginning of the Internet any more, when a copy of Photoshop and Illustrator and some nifty art skills were a quick ticket to job security.

Everyone and their mom can build a website now. You have to be good—really good—to get a job, and even then, you only get through the door by knowing someone. I know I'm good enough, but that doesn't mean it's going to be easy.

I can see the finish line. I can't slip up when I'm *this* close. *Blinders, Zoey, blinders.*

My little cricket of a conscience is trying to point out the fact that I'm in the pool house with Mr. Long Lashes, so apparently the blinders are not doing their job—but today was a 9.5 on the stress scale. I need to relax. I'll put the blinders back on the moment I step out the door.

So, if I'm here, I might as well enjoy the view. I sit down on the floral print couch and take a long sip of water.

And what a view it is.

"So, what do you do? Besides take care of small children and intimidate medical professionals?" Elliott asks, perching on the arm of the matching side chair casually.

Even in close proximity, he still keeps his distance. It's like he's trying to keep two arm lengths worth of space between us at all times. I hate it and appreciate it all at the same time. When he broke the unspoken distance rule and touched my leg today, it sent shockwaves roaring through my body.

Distance is good. My brain knows it, even if my anatomy doesn't agree with it.

I try to focus on answering his question, but I struggle to piece together an answer that's accurate but vague. That's the thing: children seep into every part of me and what I do. I don't know how to explain my life without betraying the one glaring detail I've managed to keep tucked away in my own little fireproof safe in the back corner of my mind. Even massive destruction won't let that shit out.

So, I start with the only thing that is the most me. "I draw—or design, I guess. I'm about to finish up my classes for my degree in graphic design and development."

"That's awesome. You code?" Elliott's eyes light up, and I feel the urge to say or do anything to keep that look glued to his face.

"Just some front-end stuff, but eventually I'd like to learn some back-end development too."

"The best designer I worked with in Cali was this crazy artistic chick who could design and build a website from start to finish in hours. I tried to hire her when I started my company, but I couldn't compete with the salary she was already making. It's a killer combo to be able to do both."

Oh yeah. Elliott was in the tech world out on the West Coast; I forget that. He looks more ready for a pickup game of basketball than some twenty-four-hour hack-a-thon. West Coast tech screams hoodies, fitness tracking bracelets, and one perma-cuffed pant leg from riding a bike everywhere.

Something about Elliott doesn't fit my image of Silicon Valley —maybe because he fits here.

I can't stifle my curiosity. "Why'd you leave?"

In one swift movement, Elliott is up from the chair, one of his hands reaching back around his neck and then absentmindedly scratching the short trim of hair just behind his ears.

Would it be weird if I got up, walked right over to him, and touched his hair? *That deliciously ruffled hair...* Yeah, definitely weird.

"It didn't work out." Elliott's voice is strained, like someone pulled his vocal chords taut, causing the vibration to be quick and metallic.

I want to ask why. Did his job not turn out like he thought it would? Was the city too crowded or hectic or overwhelming? Did he just miss home?

Did he get his heart broken?

My own chords tighten at the thought, which makes me want to smack myself. I barely know this guy, and I have absolutely no claim over the state of his love life. There is no reason I should have a physical reaction to the idea of him in love with another woman.

He should date all the women. Sleep with all the ladies. Swipe right to his heart's content.

A voice on a megaphone in my brain shouts out, *Or just sleep with you.*

It is now my life mission to track down the internal megaphone, burn it, and spread the ashes in half a dozen different places so there is no hope of a zombie resurrection.

I can sympathize with Elliott though, and it's making me feel connected in our shared vulnerability. Life didn't work out the way we expected. When you're handed a sharp right turn, it takes a while to move forward. You just fumble along trying to figure out where you are and if you need to, or even can, reroute.

"I don't think I could have moved to the other side of the country and built a life for myself. I hate to admit it, but I'm one of those who was born here, raised here, and is probably going to live here forever. I can't help it. It's who I am." Sometimes I wish I were different, times when I feel like all the friends I grew up with move forward at warp speed and I'm stuck here at turtle pace. I look over at Elliott, wishing he would catch my eyes so he could see how much I mean what I say. "I admire what you did. I wish I was brave enough to do something like that."

Elliott finally looks back at me from his spot near the glass door that faces the marbled water. For someone who looks so put together, who comes off as confident and relaxed, there's something tucked deep in there that's broken. I wish I could fix it. I wish trying to fix it wasn't such a risky proposition.

"I don't think there was very much about what I did that was brave." He shakes his head. "I just ran fast—from things, toward things—until I couldn't any more, and now I'm here, crashing at my sister's pool house."

I never would have guessed that hidden under that easy bravado was shame, but it's as clear as the crease between his eyebrows. I want to press my lips to that wrinkled sliver of skin, but life isn't a fairytale. I can't make his problems disappear with a kiss. Whatever they are, he's going to have to work through them piece by piece.

I know a little something about that deep-in-the-trenches work. "It's not as bad as the voice in your head is telling you it is."

Elliott wraps his hand around the back of his neck and strains his head back with a deep exhale. "You don't know that."

I shake my head in disagreement. "Whatever it is, I know you're a good person."

Elliott's eyebrow ticks up and his gaze intensifies. I feel like I might disintegrate.

"Even if I am, I don't always do the right thing." His voice is husky, and I get the feeling we're not talking about the problems that led him here any more.

I blink quickly. Maybe I'm imagining it. "What makes you say that?"

"I think about you more than a good person should."

My mouth goes completely dry. I'm not imagining it. I should run away from this conversation, like I'm the virgin in a horror film. They always get screwed—and not in a good way—but I'm drawn in. I can't stop myself.

"You do?" It's as much a confirmation as it is a question.

Elliott pushes off against the door frame and takes a step toward me, his hand still wrapped behind his head.

"Yeah, I do." He swallows slowly. "I like you. A good person would walk away and leave you alone, but I'm two steps away from kissing you—and damn, I really want to."

I can't breathe. My lungs refuse to let go of the air they just pulled in. They're stuck in place, thoroughly and completely shut down in surprise. My brain is slowly whispering *This is a bad idea* over and over while fumbling for the reset button. Even in the midst of the decreasing levels of oxygen available, it's not all that convincing. My brain finally finds the big red button the moment I hear a car engine pull into the driveway.

I'm suddenly up from the couch and over to the door in a matter of nanoseconds. As I reach for the handle, I bump into the warm skin of Elliott's forearm and my lungs stutter momentarily at the contact. I mumble an apology and yank the door open with such force that I nearly lose my balance. I hear a chuckle but don't dare look back as I race toward the main house doors.

Elliott follows me, stepping through the threshold just as the garage door closes and Samantha dashes in, her face flushed.

"You haven't been answering your phone. Where's Stewart?" She's practically screaming.

I instinctively reach for my back pocket, feeling the familiar rectangular outline of my phone. *Crap.* "I'm sorry, I turned it on silent when I put Stewart down for a nap. He's upstairs still. Everything's okay. He's okay."

Samantha takes a deep breath, but I can't tell if it's to soothe the fire in her lungs or to prepare to unleash the flames on me with brutal force.

Elliott steps forward from his spot behind me and shifts so that half of his frame is covering mine. I want to pause time and take in his wide shoulders and the close-up view of the strong lines that make their way down to his tapered waist. Even covered in a cotton t-shirt, it's clear there is a thick layer of muscle covering every inch of that landscape.

Considering I'm in the room with a dragon who's deciding if she's going to breathe fire or not, it's not exactly the time to get distracted.

"We tried to get ahold of you." Elliott's voice is calm, but there's a thread of strength running through the core of the statement: *We* tried. He's both implicating himself and also wrapping me with a sturdy blanket of protection from the lick of the flames.

"You didn't try hard enough," Samantha snaps. I can practically hear her teeth gnashing together in their hunt for blood.

"We did try. Your assistant was a little…" Elliott pauses. "Obstinate. I don't think she wanted to go against your no-interruptions rule."

"It's my child," she replies pointedly. I know that voice. I can hear the shift in the dragon fire; it's turned on its owner, and it's starting to burn her from the inside.

What kind of mother are you if you weren't even there for your child when they needed you? You're not good enough. You're not enough. You're a failure.

I know that voice. I've met it in the dark corners of motherhood, the ones we don't acknowledge even exist, much less talk about.

I step to the side, out from behind Elliott's frame. "Stewart's okay. I overreacted. He fell in the pool because he got excited and he bumped his back. We got multiple, very educated opinions and many tests, and it's just a bruise and some swelling. He missed his typical afternoon nap window and he was exhausted when we got home so I put him down. He's going to love having you for some cuddles when he wakes up."

I see the bright red color fade from Samantha's cheeks, and her stance softens. When she doesn't immediately respond, I take a deep breath. Crisis averted—for the second time today.

"Okay, I'm going to head out. I'll see you tomorrow." I look to see if she's okay with me going.

Samantha nods and walks out toward the front entrance, probably to check the mail then head upstairs. I managed to put the dragon to rest, but it doesn't mean we're about to have a motherhood heart-to-heart and braid each other's hair. I'm an employee. I serve a purpose, and that's my only function to her.

My bag is still on the counter from when we got home from the doctor's office. I pick it up and reach in for my car keys. "See you tomorrow."

Elliott looks confused. I think he's still trying to catch up with how I managed to defuse the situation.

Mom magic, that's how, but there's no way I can explain that. So, I just smile and make my way toward the door, trying to permanently imprint the image of him stepping in front of me like some Hercules, ready to protect me from the mythical beast.

Little does he know, I'm no damsel in distress.

Chapter 14

Elliott

I don't think I've actually sat down with just my sister since before I went to college, and that conversation only lasted about five minutes. So, it's eerie to sit down with a beer in hand at the kitchen island across from Sam tonight. When I offered to help with Stewart's bedtime and she gladly accepted—unlike every other night where she practically exiles me to my poolside retreat —I knew something was up.

Sam comes off as a hard-ass thanks to years of training from our dad. He wasn't going to let his first child take a backseat in life, and he sure as hell wasn't going to let something as simple as gender keep her from getting into the most elite boardrooms in corporate law. I know better though. She was shaken up today, and even though she'd never admit it, she needs someone around to calm her down—well, someone, and a very large, very expensive glass of red wine.

"Stewart's a really cute kid. Strange, but cute." I open our conversation with a safe topic. Sam loves her son more than anything else in the world. She's a big marshmallow when it comes to Stewart. You wouldn't know it, but that's because not many people get to see the two of them together.

Sam twirls the thin stem of her glass between her fingertips. "He's not strange."

I raise my eyebrows. "Do you remember what I was like when I was three?"

"Yes, you were annoying as hell. You jumped off everything in sight and wanted to listen to Van Halen all the time."

Okay, so maybe I am not the best judge of strange. "He's just so calm for a three-year-old. He doesn't have temper tantrums. He sits and colors. He cleans up his plate after meals—without being asked."

Sam lifts her shoulders as if to ask if I expected anything less; I guess I didn't. I knew Stewart would be an incredible kid. It pissed me off when his dad left just months after he was born, but that guy was a jerk from the start. I still don't know why my sister married him in the first place.

"You've got good help." This earns a piercing look. "What?" I respond with mock helplessness.

"Stay away from my nanny," Sam warns. Even though Sam was well into her law school years when I started high school, she still heard about all the girls I dated back then. Sixteen was a good year for me. License plus keys to Dad's BMW was gold.

"What are you talking about?" I know exactly what she's talking about. I walked in today with every intention of keeping Zoey and I in the friend zone, and if Sam hadn't showed up, I would have blown that plan to pieces. I'm sure as hell not going to admit that though.

"I'm not stupid. I see the way you look at her. I'm being nice letting you crash here, especially without telling Mom and Dad," she says with a hint of blackmail.

Part of me wants to tell her making Zoey off limits is more dangerous than just leaving it alone, but it's not worth pushing. "You don't have to worry about it. I'm not on the market." I don't add that Zoey deserves someone better than a jobless freeloader.

Sam stares at me as if she's scanning my face for any hint of a lie. She stops and takes a drink of wine. Apparently, I pass inspection.

"So, what about your market? Been on any dates lately?" I ask, knowing full well I'm pushing buttons, but sometimes you have to rile them up over nothing in order to calm them down about something. Sam just glares at me.

"Come on, you've got a nanny. Isn't there some dating site for lawyers anyway? If there isn't, maybe I should make one. There's probably a market for that." I think about it for a second while Sam mentally turns my face into a dartboard. "Although, I'd probably get sued. A lot. Good thing I've got plenty of legal counsel in the family."

"I am not going to be your lawyer."

"Who said I was asking you?"

"Dad's sure as hell not going to be your lawyer either." Fair, and I would eat dog food dipped in sewer water before ever asking him for a favor like that. I won't even crash at his house while he's not there, and my mom can't keep a secret to save her life. There's no way I could have asked her without inadvertently asking my dad too.

"Fine, I won't start a dating site for lawyers—doesn't mean you shouldn't double-check that there isn't one out there already." It may be pushing buttons, but it's true nonetheless. My sister would be happier if she had someone to share her time with —well, someone who doesn't go to bed at 8:00pm and drink whole milk in a plastic cup with their dinner.

Sam ignores the second half of my statement, but I can tell by the look in her eyes that she is latching onto the first part. "What are you going to do next?"

"I have no idea." I wish I knew, but I can't begin to imagine starting another company, although it's even worse imagining myself going to a bunch of interviews and turning my experience into the uplifting and insightful bullshit everyone wants to hear. Thinking about it makes me want to punch a wall. Something tells me random aggression is not one of those traits that wins you a follow-up round of interviews.

"Well, don't get too comfortable here. I'm kicking you out the second you cross the line from temporarily needing a place to stay over into full-on mooch." She finishes the last of her wine in a tilted sip and hops off the stool. "I need to go wash my face and then read through some briefs before bed."

It's only nine. I'd like to say my night is just starting, but I'm probably one more beer and a few Netflix clicks away from going to sleep. I'd be embarrassed if it didn't sound like exactly what I had planned when I bought my one-way ticket here.

I need to zone out for a while before I can wake up and be a real adult again.

Out of the corner of my eye, I see Sam turn around just before she reaches the doorway. "Thanks for your help today."

"Anytime. I'd jump in front of a bus for that kid." I may not be his dad, but that doesn't stop me from feeling like my job as his uncle is any less important.

Sam nods. It's rare for her to show appreciation. She may give me crap about showing up on her doorstep, but I know it's valuable to her for me to be here. I have to admit, it's nice to be needed. After everything in California, this is exactly where I need to be.

Chapter 15

Zoey

I arrive home to a living room full of tulle and tiaras, and I know immediately that my sister is home. I hear giggling from the girls' bedroom and make my way down the hall toward it. My sister has a blanket wrapped around her legs and a bra on over her vintage Beatles t-shirt. She seems to be doing a mash-up rendition of songs from *The Little Mermaid* with slightly off-key accompaniments from the twins. What can I say? Cassie is the only one of us who scored the gift of pitch.

I'm content to stand in the hallway and peek in on the happy homecoming festivities, but Louisa's hearing is better than a trained watchdog.

"Mom!" she cries out, turning to the door and flinging it all the way open. I bend down to catch her in my arms for a tight squeeze and Phoebe piles on.

Leaving them in the morning can feel like I'm pulling my heart out of my chest with my bare hands and setting it on the counter until I get home. They get just a little bit older every day, and sometimes it really feels like I'm missing it.

But, I wouldn't give up these hugs for the whole world. Their joy is as tangible as the feeling of running barefoot in the grass on the sunniest of days.

They're happy to have me home, just like I'm happy to have Cassie home. I untangle myself from their tiny arms and rush over to wrap my arms around her. No matter what the circumstances are, I would take her home any day of the week.

"Someone had to come home and teach these girls vintage Disney…the best Disney." Cassie is poking a sleeping beast, and one look at the smile on her face tells me she knows what she's doing.

"But what about Elsa and Anna?" Phoebe cries out.

"Sister power forever!" Louisa backs her up.

Oh, Cassie Porter, causing trouble wherever she goes.

"All I'm saying is you don't get a perfectly crafted Alan Menken score every day. *The Little Mermaid* was genius." Cassie's fingers are stretched out wide, as if she's ready to catch the amazingness of the music right in the palms of her hands.

Phoebe and Louisa both cry out in protest, and their tiny voices meld together to create one high-pitched flurry of noise.

I thought we'd finally gotten past *Frozen* on constant repeat, but I'm pretty sure Cassie just reignited the lingering flame with a blowtorch.

Sure enough, my mini speakers are retrieved and the Porter women "Let It Go" all through dinner prep. I take the mental cue and try to banish thoughts of Elliott to the furthest edge of my brain. Every time my brain replays what he said tonight, my eyes go wide and I feel rooted in place, too stunned to move a single muscle.

By bath time, we've moved on to the musical delights of *Tangled*. At some point, my mom sneaks out for her weekly book club. I'm pretty sure book club is just a reason for her group of mom friends to get together and drink, but hey, if I had free time, you know I'd do the same thing. So, Cassie and I tackle the bedtime routine together.

Just as I'm turning down the dimmer on the nightlight, Louisa whispers sleepily, "Aunt Cassie should be the next Disney princess. She'd be the best."

I smile to myself. She would be the best. Porter women are strong women, and I wish every little girl had role models like my mom and sister. When I turn around to leave the girls' room, I see Cassie in the doorway. Judging by the smile on her face, she knows how big a compliment Louisa just gave her.

I sneak out and shut the door, motioning for Cassie to follow me. There's a bottle of wine with our name on it. We take it out to the screened-in porch and listen to the chorus of crickets and toads.

"So, you're home…" I say. I'm not going to tiptoe around and talk about how great the weather is. My sister is home for the summer when she had planned to be in LA.

"Yeeeaaah." She breathes her word out like it's been sitting on her tongue for hours. She follows it up with a long pull at the bottle of white. Porter family rule: if it's twist-off, no glass is necessary. We're cheap and lazy in all the right ways. "I needed to get out."

Cassie passes the bottle and I take my own long sip. Yup, I know that feeling.

"I thought the semester was going really well," I say. It's half statement, half question. Cassie went out to UCLA on a scholarship for swimming, and after studying biology nonstop for a year, she took a drama class to add something a little less about science and a little more about reading and interpreting. She loved it and excelled so quickly that she switched majors and went for it. My sister, the natural drama queen; who would have guessed?

"It was. I mean, it did go well. Academically. There was just this one instructor. He just…" She trails off.

"Was an ass?" I want to beat him up instantly.

"Not exactly." Even in the dim glow of the twinkle lights hung around the perimeter of the screens, I can tell Cassie is turning red—scarlet red.

"Oh my god, did you sleep with your professor?!" My exclamation is followed by more blushing and a long sip of wine.

"No," she finally counters. "I wanted to though. We kept running into each other. His dad is a big shot director, producer guy, so he's at all the parties, my agent's office, auditions. It was getting to be ridiculous."

Sounds like we both have a little problem with men who are clearly off limits.

"But you're done for the semester. Couldn't you hook up with him now that the course is done?"

Cassie sighs. "He's teaching two of my classes next semester. I know it's LA and everyone sleeps with everyone, I just don't want to start off like that. I want to do this right. I want to make it because I'm good, not because I'm easy. You know?"

LA is a different planet. Cassie would get jobs from putting out; I'd lose mine. The irony is not lost on me, but I respect my sister for her integrity. She is a phenomenal actress, and I plan on being her very subpar red carpet arm candy. I fully admit I am not a Chris—Evans, Pratt, Pine, or otherwise—but I'll be there until she has a Chris of her own.

"So your vagina ran you out of town?" I deadpan.

Embarrassment fades to giggles. "That, and I went to a bunch of auditions and didn't land a single part for the summer. Any auditions now would be for the fall, and I only have two more semesters. I want to see my degree through. So, if I'm going to be a waitress, I might as well be around my amazing sister and her rock-star daughters."

"Point taken. We are pretty awesome."

"Which brings me to my proposition for the evening." Cassie wags her eyebrows dramatically.

Uh oh. Cassie has had many propositions over the years: trying our own bang trims—mediocre success for her, disaster for me; covering our principal's yard in toilet paper—detention for a month AND cleanup duty. I'm not hopeful that this will be any better.

Cassie hands me the bottle and I feel the strong urge to guzzle the rest before her big reveal. "Remember, I have two children who depend on me. This can't involve potential jail time."

"Oh, way less risk. I think we should set up a dating profile for you."

My brain first jumps to Elliott and then to those weird dating site commercials that are supposed to be footage of real dates.

Yeah, I'm not signing up for that level of awkward of my own accord. No, thank you. My vibrator doesn't have awkward pauses, and I get all the same benefits.

"I can tell by your silence you need to think about it, but I think it's a really good time for it," she says.

"Yeah, my silence was thinking about the fifty ways to say *hell no*, and there's no good time for online dating."

"Come on." I can tell by her tone that one third of a bottle of wine is still more than enough to get my sister tipsy.

"Not gonna happen. Between work all day, the girls, and summer classes, I have no time."

And there's the glaring fact that I'm hopelessly attracted to the most eligible, most attractive option I've ever come across. That does not give me much hope for finding a better candidate on a site full of optimistically flattering pictures and carefully crafted bios that talk about loving long walks and Cinnamon Toast Crunch cereal. *Yeah dude, we all like those things.*

This whole conversation is strange. Cassie and I never talked about our love lives when we were younger, and it's not like I've been playing the heart-shaped field these days.

"But I can help watch the girls," Cassie pleads.

"Uh uh, not happening, and if I so much as get a hint that

you're making a profile for me, I will personally release every single embarrassing home video of you faster than you can say YouTube famous."

Cassie sighs in defeat, and I'm satisfied that my threat is taken seriously.

Even though she's talking about something that sounds worse than sticking my feet in piranha-infested water, I know she's doing it out of love. I look over at her and I'm overwhelmed with gratitude. "I'm glad you're home. You're my favorite sister in the whole world."

"I'm your only sister." She sticks her tongue out to the side in mock disapproval.

"Hey, we have a parent at large. You don't know what kind of half-siblings we've got rolling around out there."

Cassie laughs, a full rumble that starts at her core and shakes all the way up to her cheeks. "Fair. We have no idea how much of a horn-dog Dad really is."

"Exactly, and I don't care how great they may be. They could be curing cancer and you'd still be my favorite."

Cassie just smiles and leans over, dropping her head onto my shoulder. Hell, even if we weren't sisters, I'd still choose Cassie. Every single time.

Chapter 16

Elliott

I managed to get out of the house for the entire day after the pool incident, but I haven't been able to drag the image of Zoey in that pink bikini from its current location at front and center in my mind. My willpower is shot.

Someone once told me if you're craving something sweet, just eat some protein. When your body craves sugar, it's low on fuel and needs a boost. I think they were referencing doughnuts at the time, but hey…

Well, I ate about ten protein bars yesterday, and all it did was make me shit a brick this morning.

I give up. I can't avoid that face or the way her hair starts to come undone from her ponytail around it. I definitely can't not check out her butt for another second. I'm a gentleman, not a saint.

I skip the lunchtime basketball game with my buddies because today I have a plan.

I know better than to sneak into the main house while my sister's still home. She's a lawyer, which means she gets paid buckets of cash to ask a lot of questions and sniff out lies. I don't need to wave a red cape in front of a professional bull. She already gave me a warning; I don't need to prove her right.

So, I wait until I hear one car pull up and a second car pull away. I don't want to lose my opportunity, and in the world of kids, you're always just one nap and a snack time away from bad timing.

When I walk in the door, I can hear Stewart at the kitchen counter asking about their plans between mouthfuls of some ten-dollars-a-box cereal that earns me dirty looks from my sister when I call it Cheerios.

I make my way through the hallway and emerge in the kitchen with a wide grin and a printout in my hands. "Why don't we go to the hands-on museum today?"

I can see Stewart's face explode in tiny toddler happiness like I just declared it's both Christmas AND his birthday today. Zoey turns around to face me. I can tell she's confused by my sudden involvement in their day-to-day, but she doesn't seem upset by the change.

Good; that means I was right: I have a shot here.

Surprise fades to logistics. "It's going to take us a bit to get out of here. We need to finish breakfast first." Zoey reaches down to play with his hair while she continues to think through the steps. I would trade my killer jump shot to switch places with the kid. "Okay. Then we need to get you dressed, and I need to grab snacks and your sunscreen and probably your swimsuit."

My throat constricts at the thought of adding swimsuits to the mix. This is starting to seem like my best idea ever. I was brilliant and didn't even realize it.

"They have this awesome splash area," Zoey explains as she looks up at me. "Stewart always gets soaked."

Okay, hold off on the awards for smartest man alive. If it's a splash zone, then it's probably not swimsuits for all of us, just Stewart. The idea is still pretty solid though. Stewart is ruin-the-potty-training-and-pee-his-pants levels of excited, and this idea means spending the whole day together. I don't have to linger around the house for a word or two here and there.

I'm done trying to avoid Zoey. I'm captivated by this woman who can both hold her own with my sister and take care of Stewart like some fantastical hybrid of Mary Poppins and Scarlett Johansson.

I've spent the last few years around women who focused too much on money—whether I had it or some venture capitalist predicted I would have it—or were on their own 24/7 startup gig that left no room for anything other than Powerbars for lunch and coffee dates to talk strategy. Seriously, I once asked a girl out on a date and we ended up at some hipster Starbucks knockoff drinking something that tasted like burnt gasoline, and all she wanted to talk about was where she saw our companies in the next five years. It was like having a date with my business analyst, and he rocked a skinny jean better than half the women on the West Coast.

I'm a Carolina boy. When you take a girl on a date, you talk about how you grew up and what kind of books you like. You act like a gentleman, but you sure as hell take a damn long look when she gets up to use the ladies' room.

I plan on doing a lot of that today. This is a date, whether Zoey knows it or not.

Chapter 17

Zoey

I've never known what it's like to have a man around to help.

I've worn it like some unspoken badge of honor—single mom of twins, nanny of a toddler, unofficial badass with two X chromosomes—but today felt like sinking into a deep, broken-in leather armchair. Elliott was right there in the thick of each hands-on exhibit with Stewart and me, plugging in the giant Lite-Brite bulbs to make a geometric smiley face, climbing through the indoor rope jungle gym, moonwalking through the bubble room.

It's frighteningly attractive to watch a grown man act like a big kid just to make his nephew laugh.

We walk up to the ice cream parlor, because why the hell not when we've already crept into naptime territory? It's such a wacky day, we might as well throw in the towel and add a sugar buzz.

"Okay champ, what flavor do you want?" Elliott asks, holding Stewart up to see the two rows of fully loaded ice cream tubs. I can't help but stare at Elliott's arms, the fabric pulling against his flexed triceps.

"Chocolate, and the orange one!" Stewart points enthusiastically.

Elliott makes a face like someone just offered him green bean ice cream. Chocolate and orange creamsicle is not exactly an enticing combination. "Are you sure?" he prods gently.

"Yes." Stewart nods. Man, this kid has weird preferences, but Elliott just nods back and asks the woman behind the counter to make it a double.

"We'll share it then," he offers, and Stewart beams as if a superhero just said those were his favorite flavors too.

It makes me wonder for a split second what it would have been like if Nathan had stuck around, but I don't have to take off rose-colored glasses to know he wouldn't have been a superhero. Any man who walks away is only one evil sidekick away from villain in my book.

I step up and order a scoop of cookie dough in a waffle cone— my absolute favorite—and reach into my purse to grab my wallet.

"Oh, he already got yours," whispers the woman pulling the metal scoop against the soft slope of the ice cream with a nod toward Elliott and a sparkle in her eye that clearly implies she'd scoop his cream any day of the week.

I simultaneously want to smack her and high-five her for her good taste. I look over to sneak a peek at the fine specimen of a man who bought me my cone. *Damn, I want a scoop of him too.*

I walk over to the boys and we head outside to the park that's just two short blocks away. Stewart has already had his fill and is practically dragging Elliott in an effort to get to the playground at light speed. I silently thank Elliott for sharing, otherwise the eyes-bigger-than-the-stomach trap would have meant a half-full bowl being tossed in the trash.

I'm content to hang back and watch them, grateful for the momentary reprieve of duty. Stewart loves having his uncle around, and for a moment, I feel my guilt creeping in.

If I had tried harder, maybe my girls would have had a father. Ugh, I hate that little minion of a voice that lives in my head. I can't help it though. I know I couldn't have done anything differently to keep Nathan around, and a shitty father figure does not trump an absent one. I'd rather Phoebe and Louisa have two strong women to look up to than a self-absorbed waste of time who happens to be male.

I'm okay with how it all worked out, but seeing Elliott around Stewart doesn't help with my guilty notions of what life in some alternate perfect universe would be like—where even though I got pregnant unexpectedly, the father of my children was a true dad who made his family feel loved and supported.

When we get to the amazing playground, I let Stewart lead Elliott into the maze of life-size chutes and ladders. I take a seat on a bench and finish off my absurdly delicious cone just as I see Elliott walking over to me. I have to take a moment of grateful appreciation for the visual masterpiece in front of me. His striking physical presence is balanced by the warmth that radiates out from him.

I feel like someone crawled into my brain—or that secret

Pinterest board of absurdly attractive guys I curated and will fiercely deny ever exists—and handcrafted Elliott. I should probably go home and delete that board, just in case. I can only handle one Mr. Perfect, and even then, I'm only a hairpin's distance away from internal combustion.

Elliott sits down next to me and my internal temperature ratchets up on cue.

"Stewart found some friends." Elliott nods over to the three tiny humans happily engrossed in the giant sandbox with its various digger toys. He lets his legs open wide and leans forward so his forearms rest on the edge of his thighs. It's like he's daring me to look, saying, *Here, take this all in. I won't even pretend to notice.*

Geez, it's like someone just handed me the world's best cookie dough ice cream and then said, *Don't eat this.*

Fuck me.

"Thanks for letting me hijack your day." He stares out at the lines and curves of wood and plastic ahead of us, and his hands are gripped tightly together—too tight. I wonder what he's really thinking. "It's really nice getting to spend time with Stewart. I'm glad I'm finally getting the chance."

Does he beat himself up for not being around the past few years? I want to reach across, wrap my arms around him, and embrace his broken pieces, but I can't cross that line.

There's only a few millimeters between our legs, and it feels like my entire universe resides in that tiny breadth of space.

"Is that why you came to your sister's? Your parents aren't too far away, right?" It's a surface question, but if I dive too deep, I'm afraid I might not be able to swim back to the surface. The water will feel too good when I'm completely submerged.

Samantha's not exactly a sharing sort, but Bill and Katherine MacCallister are listed as emergency contacts, and their address is just north of Raleigh.

Elliott turns back to look at me, his eyes squinting from the sun behind me, and I'm struck by the emotion that registers in the two deep lines between his eyebrows. "Well that, and the fact that my parents are currently somewhere between Iceland and Norway. They don't know I'm back yet."

Elliott isn't as carefree as his demeanor suggests. There is more going on here, and I want to know more. *Damn you, Elliott MacCallister, with your intrigue and good looks.* He's making it impossible to stay away.

I'm so riveted by the man beside me that I don't notice the one in front of me until Elliott's focus shifts up. I hear my name. *Oh no.*

"I thought that was you!" a baritone voice interrupts happily. *Nathan.* The father of my children is standing two feet in front of me.

This is a disaster. The last time I saw Nathan was the summer I was still in my first trimester, and I was trying not to hurl from the plethora of smells at the grocery store while I picked up bagels and peanut butter—the only two food choices that sounded even remotely appetizing. He'd already made it clear he wanted nothing to do with the product of our little back-of-the-truck romp. Little did we know that product was plural. Under the horrible fluorescent lights of the store, he took one look at my slightly-pudgy-but-not-yet-recognizably-pregnant self and muttered a quick hello before turning the other way.

Oh, how times change when you've mastered the art of dry shampoo and your skinny shorts fit again.

"Hi Nathan, it's nice to see you." *No. It's not. Ugh.* I want to smack my polite southern self.

"You too. You too." He's rambling while staring squarely at Elliott, who is casually looking back and forth between Nathan and I, trying to piece the situation together.

I quickly debate whether or not to introduce them. Manners insist I do, but fuck manners. Nathan is the diabolical key to unraveling my well-organized and perfectly compartmentalized life. This conversation needs to end. Now.

I try to stand up awkwardly. Nathan is too close and I end up reaching out for his shoulders to steady myself. He thinks I'm trying to hug him and pulls me into his thick barrel chest with a tight squeeze. I catch his cheap musky scent—a horrible combination of body wash and five-dollar cologne—and I want to dry heave. I don't know how I ever found him attractive.

"We've gotta run. We brought Elliott's nephew to the park, and we've got to get home for naptime." It's a complete and utter lie, but I'll do anything to remove myself from this situation.

I give Nathan the sweetest smile I can muster and silently repeat the mantra, *Please don't screw this up*, over and over.

Nathan tilts his head to the side and his lips pinch together like he doesn't quite know what's going on, but he takes a few steps back. I can feel oxygen flooding back into my lungs. Crisis averted. He turns to walk away, but then he turns back, his mouth pulled into a thin line and his eyes narrowed in thought.

No. Don't do it. Turn back around.

"Tell the girls I say hi, okay?"

Arrrrgh. All I can think beyond every single cuss word I know and some I've made up is to keep cool. *Keep cool, Zoey Porter. Keep cool.*

Nathan walks away and I finally turn to look at Elliott, who, at some point, stood up from his seat. Points to him for going along with the naptime excuse I threw out there. His face is a mixture of amusement and confusion.

I would sacrifice chickens with my bare hands to make sure he brushes this whole encounter off.

"You look like you just got caught trying to climb out the window to get to a party." His eyes twinkle while he teases me, but he doesn't know the vein he's playing around with is the jugular.

So much for looking cool. Apparently, my brain does not communicate the message properly to, you know, all the external body parts that count. "That was just a guy I haven't seen since high school."

Oh, and the father of my two children you and your sister have absolutely no clue exist.

Elliott's expression turns serious for a split second. "An ex?"

"Yeah, I don't think Nathan is even capable of determining

relationship status without a navigation system and a twenty-four-hour supply of water. It wasn't serious." My answer seems to soften the edges of his pinched eyes. "Let's head out though. I'm sure Stewart is tired, and we need to get the sand out of his hair before your sister gets home and complains that she'll be picking up microscopic cat pee-infested granules from now until the end of summer."

Elliott nods and starts toward the sandbox, but he turns around abruptly, mirroring back the curiosity I was staring at him with just minutes before. "Who are 'the girls?'"

I wanted to dry heave just being within two feet of Nathan, but now I really do feel like I might vomit back every single speck of cookie dough delight. "Oh, just my mom and sister." I try to force my tone to stay steady, casual.

Elliott stares at me for another moment, his curiosity unflinching, before he turns back around and makes his way toward Stewart.

This is why this is a bad idea. I can't let Elliott in. I can't let him get curious. I have too much to lose if he figures out I've been hiding a massive secret this whole time.

Chapter 18

Elliott

When we get back to the car, Stewart becomes immediately engrossed in one of the picture books stashed in the back seat.

I feel like I should slip him a five or something. The kid is a perfect wingman in the making.

Zoey focuses on the road as she pulls out into traffic, and it gives me a brief moment to take in her tempting profile without being caught.

I notice a trail of freckles running up her arms and sneaking underneath the sleeve of her shirt. What I would give to follow that trail to see where it leads me.

Zoey is like a present waiting to be opened up and appreciated for years to come. She's not the type you toss to the side because you get bored. No. She's the kind you thank your lucky stars you got in the first place and do everything in your power to keep.

Which makes me wonder about this Nathan character. I have to know more.

"So you and Nathan dated in high school…" I know I'm opening up Pandora's box, but hey, curiosity made me do it.

Zoey continues to stare straight ahead at the road, and it gives me complete access to watch her bite her lip and scrunch her eyes together. I wish it were my lip she was nibbling on, and if I play my cards right, someday it will be.

"We hung out a bit," she finally answers.

"High school sweethearts, huh?" I'm teasing, even though I'm strategically interested to see her reaction to the statement.

She snorts. "Definitely not. He played basketball and I was on the dance team. We were around each other a lot, but that's all."

Somehow, I think it was a little more. Zoey's shoulders are practically up at her ears, but I'm not going to push it.

Instead, I focus on the real gem of that conversation. "You were on the dance team?"

Zoey blushes. "Yeah."

"So you can dance?"

"I can hold my own at a dance party, and I'm really good at counting to eight over and over again. That's about it."

Her shoulders relax down an inch, and I want to do everything in my power to keep that trend going. "I can't dance for anything. You'll have to teach me some of your killer dance party moves."

Zoey turns for a split second to shoot me a dubious look. "Um, I think that's something you say to throw people off. Like *Oh, I can't dance,* and then you bust out spinning on your head in the middle of the dance floor. I mean, I saw you moonwalk in the bubbles room today. It was solid."

I offer her a mock bow. "Well, thank you, but really, I have a move or two and absolutely no rhythm. It looks good until you turn some music on. Then I just look like an uncoordinated stooge. So, your counting to eight expertise sounds like it could really come in handy."

Zoey smiles, but we're interrupted as she pulls up to the subdivision gate. She rolls down the window and punches in the code.

Moments later, we pull into the driveway. Zoey pops out of the car like a lightning bolt and I scramble out to meet her as she pulls a now-sleeping Stewart out the back door.

I reach out to take him and brush her arm in the process. "Here, let me help."

Zoey recoils like she touched a live wire, and her face loses any last trace of play. "No, it's okay. I've got this."

"Are you sure?"

"Yup." She's already halfway to the door. Something is holding her back. In any other situation, I might let it go, but I felt that potent zing when I touched her arm a second ago.

I want more of that, and I have a whole summer to figure out how to get it.

Chapter 19

Zoey

By the time I get home, I'm so anxious I can practically see the tiny ants it feels like are crawling all over my skin. Great. I'm one minor catastrophe away from hallucinations.

People think mothers are these strong, badass women, like dealing with poop and screaming babies turns us into untouchable Amazonian warriors. The truth is, we learn to put on a good game face, and under that bravado is a nearly crumbling mess of self-doubt and worry.

I sit in my car for a second, trying to take deep calming breaths before I walk through the front door, and I hear a car pull up to the curb and its engine kick off. My skin prickles for an entirely different reason, and those ants morph into raised threads of hair. I jump out of my car before I have a chance to second-guess myself.

Shit.

A tall figure stands with his arms crossed over the roof of the driver side door and stares at my house.

"What are you doing here, Nathan?" I whisper, even though I

desperately want to shout. *What makes you think you can show up here?*

His eyes look tired and unsure, but I feel no pity for him—not after five years.

"I thought you still lived here. My mom mentions you sometimes."

Well, that's just a slap in the face. His mom confronted me in the grocery store when I was eight months pregnant and told me to stay away from her son. I had sent him an ultrasound picture on the off chance he was interested. Apparently, protecting her son from the harlot who dared to get pregnant was more important than actually caring about the fact that she was becoming a grandmother. I'm sure whatever language she uses when she mentions me is super affectionate.

"Yeah, and what are you doing here, exactly?" I ask pointedly, crossing my arms in case my tone doesn't get the message across. *You're not welcome here.*

Nathan sighs. Whatever he needs to say has obviously been wearing on him. I try to care for a split second, but the attempt falls flat.

"Seeing you today just brought up a lot of feelings." *Oh god, please tell me you're not about to confess your unrealized love for me.* It's like offering to make pancakes the morning after but five years later. *Dude, the sex was not that good.*

"I just…I know I haven't been part of the girls' lives, but I want them to have a father figure. I've been reading about how that's important." He clenches his jaw together as if the thought really bothers him.

I don't know whether to laugh or scream. You read a New York Times article about girls needing their fathers and suddenly you think you qualify as father material? Spoiler alert: that doesn't cut it.

I just stare at him. I'm not going out of my way to fight with him.

It doesn't stop him. "And I don't know about other men filling that role."

Other men? What other men? Oh. *Oh no you didn't*, a little voice cries out in indignation. Elliott. He's talking about Elliott being a father-like figure to the girls. Nathan has no idea that Elliott doesn't even know they exist, and I'm sure as hell not going to explain that mess of a situation.

"You don't get to have an opinion now, Nathan. Not after this many years. Not when you've never even seen their faces. You couldn't pick them out of a crowd."

"You can't say that. I'm their father. I have rights." His fists are tight.

"Yeah, well, take me to court. We'll see how far your rights go," I spit back.

It's an empty threat. I have no intention of this becoming a custody battle. I don't want to put the girls through that, and honestly, it feels like a cheap shot. I can't help it though. As far as I'm concerned, Nathan has had no interest up until this point, so he has no rights. I'm guessing the only reason he's even showing an interest now is because he saw me with another guy. He assumed we were together, so he assumed he was being replaced. Even though the first part is dead wrong, I'm not opposed to the second. Elliott is ten times the man Nathan has ever shown himself to be, and if I were going down that road, I know Elliott would be an amazing dad.

Nathan can see he doesn't have a lot of ground to stand on. He looks like a football team walk-on who showed up to practice and got his butt kicked back to the door by the defense.

I'm not going to let him win just so he can go home and feel a little better about himself.

"That's it then?" His jaw is squarely set.

"I don't know what you want me to tell you. This is the first time I've seen you in years. I don't see what's supposed to convince me you want to make an actual effort now."

"I'm here now, aren't I?" He's trying to put up a fight, but his words are starting to feel hollow.

"Too little, too late, Nathan." I shake my head. He sighs but doesn't respond. I turn on my heels and head to the side door of the house. When I pull open the screen, I hear the ignition click on and the rumble of the engine pulling away.

My mom is standing just inside the door, drying her hands off on a kitchen towel, and I can tell by the look on her face she saw something of what went down outside. Just as she starts to ask if everything is okay, two bobbing heads run up to me, shouting, "MOM'S HOME."

As I look down at two sets of my turquoise-shaded eyes staring up at me, I selfishly hope I get to continue to be their mom and dad, undisputed. I know I'm going to keep showing up, day after day, for the rest of their lives. I can shelter them from the disappointment of when a dad walks out and doesn't come back because he just couldn't any more.

Chapter 20

Zoey

When I step into the MacCallister's house the next morning, I feel like a burglar who's unsure if this is a break-in or an armed robbery; it all depends on who's currently home or not.

I have a plan, and it hinges heavily on avoidance.

I catch the alluring scent of bacon before I even make it to the kitchen, and my willpower weakens. *Damn you, stomach, you're such a whore.* I pinch my eyes together and picture Nathan walking up to us at the park. It's the image I've placed on my mental Wikipedia page of why spending time around Elliott is a really bad idea.

I'm avoiding Elliott so I can keep my job, so I can finish putting myself through school, so I can get a job that actually has vacation days and a 401k. Yeah, adulting sucks, but grownup life can't be PJs all day and Netflix binges all night. Maybe it can be for other people in their twenties, but I'm a mom. I'm pretty sure the manual they don't give you says you're supposed to make adult decisions.

I step into the kitchen and silently chant, *Be an adult, be an adult, be an adult.* Elliott is standing there in a white t-shirt that marks a perfect contrast to his tan skin. My mantra is interrupted when he flips a pancake in the air.

Literally. With some kitchen wizard voodoo, he flicks the medallion up in the air and catches it again in the hot skillet.

Be an adult.

I think he's humming underneath his breath.

Be an adult.

He turns around, opens the oven door, and bends down to peek in. The scent of crisping bacon is overpowering, but the image of Elliott's perfectly rounded ass on display in well-cut denim is the real showstopper.

Be a goddamn adult, Zoey!

I can't take this unrestricted access. I clear my throat and Elliott turns around with a smile that creeps up just a touch higher on the right side. It's like he's making extra room to display that devilish dimple. He knows exactly what I was just doing.

"I'm making breakfast." He nods toward the pancake pan.

"I can see that." I swallow, slowly. Why did you have to bring food into this, Elliott MacCallister?

"Are you interested?" The way he asks, with his eyebrows nudged up and his full, unflinching attention directed straight at me, I know what he's asking. This isn't a casual, don't even look up from what you're doing invitation to share a meal. No, this is a break the rules with me and give the powers that be a nice slow-roll middle finger sort of offer.

Too bad the powers that be in this case hold the pocketbook —or rather, the PayPal account—that pays me.

Nope. Not even bacon is worth that.

"Sorry, I already had breakfast." I shrug halfheartedly, trying to display some casual bravado. I'd give myself a pat on the back for nailing it, but I'm crazy, not stupid. "I'm sure Stewart would love some home-cooked breakfast though. I'm not really much of a cook."

Almost on cue, Stewart flies into the kitchen shouting, "BACON!" and running over to latch onto Elliott in appreciation.

Samantha isn't far behind.

"Breakfast, you interested?" Elliott asks again, not bothering to glance up.

Samantha wrinkles her nose as if he just offered her cow tongue, which is pretty much how she feels about carbs and fat. I seriously don't know what she eats. Maybe she subsists on the souls of her associates and frequently rotating assistants.

"More for you and me, kid," Elliott says to Stewart, who doesn't seem the least bit disappointed, but the smile on Elliott's face doesn't reach quite as high as it did when I first walked in the door.

Chapter 21

Elliott

By the time lunch rolls around, it's clear Zoey is avoiding me, and I have no idea why.

I wanted to build on our momentum from yesterday, so I made breakfast. I didn't really think through the fact that I've never actually seen her eat so much as an orange in the morning here, so it was more of a walk than a strike in my book. I tried to tell myself she must eat before she gets here, but then she and Stewart completely disappeared when I ran out to the pool house to get changed. Thank you, bacon grease.

Her disappearing act made it pretty clear that yesterday did not go as well as I had originally thought.

I can't figure it out. She genuinely seemed to enjoy my company. The only thing even remotely weird was her blast-from-the-past reunion. She didn't seem all that excited about the run-in. I barely said anything though, and I can't figure out how that would have cost me points.

So, when she and Stewart walk in later that afternoon, I'm ready.

"Oh man, Stewart, you look like you had a good time." I nod my head enthusiastically and he matches the movement in slow motion.

"Yeah, we went to the library and the park and the grocery store," Stewart rambles, his eyes heavy as he toddles in. "I got to eat whatever I wanted." He yawns and then smiles. "I had French fries and chicken."

I look up at Zoey, trying to make eye contact, but she continues to stare straight down at the top of Stewart's head.

"Well, it's a good thing I have your bed all ready for you. I know I would need a snooze after a good meal like that." I'm giving him a little mental nudge in the right direction, though I don't think he needs it. He just nods and slowly makes his way upstairs. I start to follow him but turn back around. "Hey Zoey, I always get the order of operations mixed up. Could you help so I don't confuse teeth brushing with book reading?"

Zoey says sure, but her arms are crossed and her lips are a flat line. It doesn't take a body language expert to confirm what I already know.

When we finally get Stewart down, I feel like I need to put a tracking device on her so I don't lose her to some secret hiding spot before I have a chance to figure out what's going on.

She heads to the kitchen and before she's even made it across the threshold, I break the silence. "So, you're avoiding me, right?"

Zoey's gaze shoots straight at me, like a perfectly arced dart. Yup, bull's-eye. "I don't know what you're talking about."

"Liar, liar, pants on fire." I wrap my arms together across my chest. I'm not backing down.

"What are you, five?" she snaps back.

I'm starting to uncover a nerve underneath the surface, and instead of heeding the caution signs, I'm reaching for it. "I could ask you the same thing. We had a good time yesterday. You enjoyed my company just as much as I enjoyed yours, but it's like I turned into some male Medusa overnight. You won't even look at me."

"I'm looking at you now, aren't I?" Her voice is strained. She doesn't want to be having this conversation, but I'm not dropping it.

I sigh loudly. "It doesn't make sense, OK? If I did something wrong, just tell me. This cold shoulder act is bullshit." My voice is rough, coming out more like kicked up gravel than I intended, and Zoey looks surprised.

She pauses and stares at me. Her arms melt from their crossed position down to her front pockets. "You're my boss's brother, and I don't think I have to explain to you that your sister isn't afraid to fire me. I need this job. I can't even begin to explain to you how much I need it. So, you're off limits. Yesterday was fun. The only thing you've done wrong is being so easy to be around. I just think we need to stay away from each other." It all tumbles out, and she ends with a heavy sigh.

"That's it? I'm likable, so you have to ignore me?" I hate her argument. I hate it because I can't argue with it.

"I'm sorry I ignored you. It's not like I have a lot of experience with weird workplace issues. It's basically Legos and making sure

108

the milk is in Stewart's favorite cup and not just the one that looks like his favorite cup." Zoey's mouth curves ever so slightly up to the left, and I want to run over and kiss that plump crescent moon of hers.

She's right about my sister. I'm not entirely sure Sam wouldn't try to disown me for causing her to fire a good nanny and creating hours of additional work trying to find a replacement. I'd be disowned and billed for hours.

I know it's a risk, but sometimes you have to take off all your clothes, jump into the water, and just trust that no one is going to steal your shit. I don't know how I'm going to convince Zoey of that, but it doesn't mean I'm giving up.

"Okay," I finally reply, thankful that at least she was honest.

"I'll stop ignoring you," she says. Her tone is friendly, but her face is serious. "I just need space, okay?"

"As in, say, two feet? Would that be sufficient?"

This time, I'm greeted with a smile. "If I can smell your body wash, I don't think it counts as space."

"Note to self, get unscented body wash."

This earns me a full laugh.

Zoey Porter, you don't know it yet, but from here on out, I'm going to spend every single minute I can trying to make you laugh again. And again. And again.

Chapter 22

Zoey

I think I need to break up with my brain. It's going crazy and dragging me down with it.

I showed up at the MacCallister's house today and found that Elliott has gone on some boys' trip, something about fishing. When I asked for how long, Stewart had no idea. For a sliver of a second, I was almost mad at the kid. How dare he not find out exactly how long his uncle would be gone and remember that tiny detail?

Then I remembered that Stewart is three and I'm a lunatic. My job is easier when Elliott isn't around, remember? Hell, I asked him for space, and going on a fishing trip is doing exactly what I asked for.

So do you know what I thought about all day?
Elliott.
Do you know what I tried to think about all day?
Anything but Elliott.
Do you think that worked for even a second?
Hell to the no.

Thank goodness I have a new class starting tonight. I went home for dinner, grabbed my laptop and sketch pad, and raced out for the night class. Focusing on school and a subject area I actually like seems like the perfect prescription to snap out of Elliott-mania.

Because let's be honest here, I am that girl. You know, the one who sits up front with five pens laid out and notes perfectly outlined in 1 2 3, a b c, I II III style. I'm the one who actually takes advantage of office hours and reads the assignment—the whole thing, not just the first and last paragraphs. Don't hate. I got pregnant at eighteen. I don't have time to be the half-asser in the back row who is barely scraping by.

I'm so close. I won't be a nanny going to night school any more. I won't be working at a job I fell into. I'll be doing something that challenges and excites me. I have to acquire said job first, but hey, motivation!

My mind flickers to Elliott. He won't be off limits once I'm done being a nanny, but my brain doesn't have time to contemplate that possibility. The professor walks up to the table at the front of the room and hooks his computer up to the tangle of cords. The giant screen behind him flicks to life, and someone hits the lights.

He runs us through his bio—impressive—and the class particulars like grade composition and major assignments—boring but useful.

And then he starts what he calls "the good part," the reason we're sitting in this lecture hall: the interpretation and

111

representation of graphic designs. He flicks through a handful of images, some web design, some advertisements, a book cover, then asks us what they have in common.

Nothing that makes sense. There isn't a graphic theme or pattern to the group. Classmates raise their hands, offering guesses, but he shakes his head no to each theory. Then, he points to someone just behind me, and I turn around to see the familiar face of a girl who's been in a few of my classes.

She clears her throat. "Relationships. Each example drew on a relationship in its design. Parenthood. Romance. Coworkers. Neighbors. Whether it predominantly showed the actual relationship or not, it used emotions and social norms associated with them to achieve a desired effect."

The professor claps his hands together in delight. "Exactly! As designers, we are artists with a purpose." He pauses to let the idea sink in. It's true; my favorite part of this job is using my artistic abilities to turn ideas into something beautiful and useful.

He turns off his laptop and turns up the lights before continuing. "We are creating visual tools to achieve a specific goal or set of goals. Relationships are the foundation of our work, so I encourage you to use your own as the first level of study in this course. Understanding how we, ourselves, as well as the people around us think, feel, and act in our relationships is tantamount to interpreting, understanding, and achieving outstanding graphic design."

I should be thinking about how my lens as a mother, a daughter, a sister, and a friend relates to my interpretation of design—those would make the most sense—but no, I'm sitting here thinking about how I wouldn't mind a romantic lens with the one man who is one hundred percent totally and completely not allowed.

I should wear a rubber band on my wrist so I can snap myself every time my mind drifts to the boy in the pool house.

It's a losing battle until I hear the words competition and internship, and I notice flyers are being handed out down each row.

It's a call to reimagine our school's website for a chance to win a paid internship with the school's design department. *Paid!* The cynic in me knows it's an easy way to get good ideas for free, but the opportunist in me doesn't care as long as the offer is legit. I need to find a job after school ends, and a paid internship would not be a bad way to kick off my resume.

The deadline is in two weeks. I don't have much time, but I'm going to make it work. I know I can do it.

Chapter 23

Elliott

Zoey asked for space, and I've been trying to give it to her. At first, it was hard to sit in the pool house and think about her hanging out a hundred yards away from me. I needed to get away, so when Brandon mentioned a fishing trip, I immediately said yes. I escaped temptation for a few days, but desire never even left the building. At least it gave me some time to come up with a new plan. The first part involves getting my own shit together. The second part involves winning her over.

I set down my laptop and it's a million tabs of job openings and used car searches. I need a break. I'm sick of looking for what you can buy for $500. I've narrowed that answer down to a hubcap and half a dashboard. The job search isn't coming along much better.

I need a snack, which works well with part two of my plan. You'll never succeed at convincing a girl to date you by badgering her. Nope. You have to remind her that you exist from time to time in a very informal and low stakes way, and you work your way in slowly.

Thank you, stomach, for being the perfect cover.

As I make my way toward the French doors of the house, I see the outline of Zoey's blonde hair pulled up into a messy bun on the top of her head, threads coming loose at the back where her head meets her neck. I wish I could walk right in and kiss that sweet exposed curve of skin. Even if I had to wait until Stewart doesn't need a nanny, I'm betting the wait would be worth it.

I need a moment to pull myself together before I walk through those doors. If all I can think about is what it would be like to kiss her, I'll sound like an incoherent fool.

This is the long game, bro.

Zoey snaps around the moment I open the doors. She gives me an uneasy smile. I swear if she hadn't told me I was off limits last week, I'd think she didn't like me. Instead, that conversation fueled my hope. If she didn't like me, she wouldn't be telling herself to stay away. I have a shot, and that tiny little glimmer of hope has made me happier than any experience I sought out on the opposite coast.

"I'm just getting a snack. Stewart's sleeping?" I make eye contact and wish I could sit and sink into those clear tropical tide pools of hers, but we're not there yet. So, I quickly move into the kitchen.

Zoey nods, and I notice she has an editor open and what looks like the image of a website to the side.

I open the fridge and grab an apple and some of the surprisingly delicious almond butter Sam keeps stocked in the fridge. On my way back through, I always make it a point to ask a question or two. I'm genuinely curious, so it's easy to slip in a few here and there, slowly prying Zoey back open after her self-imposed shutdown.

"What are you working on?" I walk up to the table and try to get another look at her screen.

Zoey's hand hovers over the top of her screen, about to close away her project. Something tells me it's more about being self-conscious of her work than wanting to stop and focus on having a conversation with the forbidden fruit.

I smile and take a bite of my apple.

"Just a project for class. Well, a competition really." Zoey barely finishes her sentence before she's interrupted by the guitar strums of her phone ringing. She glances at the screen and frowns. "I need to take this." I nod and she slips out the back door, pressing the phone to her ear.

I take the opportunity to step closer to her computer and sneak a peek at the design docked on the right. It's only a fraction of the page, but from what I can see, it's really solid. Incredible illustrations. Easy navigation. Good color and font choices. It makes me want to see more, but I hear the door open before I can take in the rest.

Zoey's cheeks flush when she realizes what I'm looking at. She quickly moves toward the table and snaps the computer shut.

I want to tell her I liked it, but I constantly feel like I'm backing a skittish cat into a corner. It doesn't matter if I hold out a treat or not, I worry I'm going to scare her back into hiding under the couch. I resign myself to heading back to the pool house. I can try again tomorrow.

"Um, that was my sister." Zoey's voice surprises me—it's hesitant. "She was at an interview nearby and needs to print off some more resumes before she hits up a couple restaurants downtown." It's a statement with the lift of a question at the end.

Ah, I get it. I address her unspoken concern. "I'm not going to run and tell my sister you had a visitor. Besides, Stewart's napping."

Zoey's shoulders roll back down. "Okay, it won't take long. She'll be in and out."

Not two minutes later, a car engine idles outside before shutting off. I manage to loiter around the kitchen. I wouldn't dare pass up the chance to meet another Porter. Siblings have all the good information: the embarrassing stories, the map to the Achilles heel, the dirt on the competition. It's always in your best interest to make friends with the siblings.

Hell, Sam may not be my best friend, but I'm sure she has enough dirt on me to make the FBI blush.

Zoey is already at the front door and two voices start going back and forth in hushed tones. My heartbeat notches up in tempo. I want her sister to like me. I want the family seal of approval.

Finally, they make their way back to the kitchen. For the quickest of seconds, I'm thrown for a loop. A version of Zoey who is nearly as tall as me walks in wearing black skinny jeans and a white blouse.

She looks pretty surprised to see me too. I'm disappointed for a second when I realize Zoey must have never mentioned me.

"Hi, I'm Cassie." She offers out her hand. "Nice to meet you." I can tell she's sizing me up, but the way she looks at me is less about attraction and more about scoping me out.

"I'm Elliott. I hear you're in town from LA for the summer."

"Yeah, the actress-working-as-a-waitress field is a little oversaturated out there," she deadpans. I guess a sense of humor runs in the Porter line. "Where did you come from?" she adds.

"Your sister didn't tell you?"

"I didn't even know you existed." Cassie's eyebrows rise up an inch. "Which is very interesting." She adds a fraction of a smile, like she's just uncovering an interesting secret. Zoey's eyes grow wide. It is interesting, very interesting.

"I came from the opposite end of California a few weeks ago," I answer.

"A few weeks, huh? Well, if my sister doesn't snatch you up, I will," Cassie says with a straight face that breaks into a comical grin she flashes straight at Zoey. I guess I'm not the only one who likes to mess with their siblings' buttons. Zoey looks like she could hulk out at any second as her nostrils flare and her hands ball into tight fists. "Well, I gotta print my resumes and run. It was nice to meet you, Elliott."

I watch the two of them head toward the home office up front that has a massive printer. I just got an extra boost of confidence that I'm on the right path.

Chapter 24

Zoey

"What the hell just happened?" I snap. I know I'm overreacting, but no matter how many times I repeat that in my head, I can't seem to slow down the speeding train of emotions. Cassie may be the actress, but I'm being the drama queen. She looks at me with clear disapproval. She is not interested in dealing with my crazy parts.

"I was just joking." She waves her hand like she's halfheartedly batting away a fruit fly.

"You don't joke about dating my boss's brother if I don't do it first—TO HIS FACE." I'm practically shaking. I can feel my breath vibrating angrily against my nostrils as I try to pull it in.

"He thought it was funny. You're the only one who's upset over this." She tosses the resumes into the passenger seat haphazardly, not bothering to give my temper tantrum any more attention. It's everything I can do to not pull those resumes right back out and throw them on the ground like a scorned child.

I settle for verbal anger. "You crossed a line—actually about ten thousand flashing neon lines. I can't believe you did that. You can't joke like that where I work."

Cassie turns back to me and tips her head to the side, as if she's studying me from a different angle. Her eyes squint in the bright summer sun, but she looks cool as a cucumber. "So, you're pissed off that I somehow made you seem unprofessional by acknowledging that the guy who lives here is off-the-charts attractive and totally dating material?"

"Yes." I fling the word back forcefully before I can even think through what Cassie's getting at, but when she begins to grin, I regret the hard emphasis of my reply.

"So, you think he's hot." It's a statement, not a question.

Ugh. "Fine. Yes. He's attractive. Any woman would agree with me." I cross my arms defiantly, and then I immediately uncross them. Every overreaction is just handing Cassie another piece of the puzzle.

"I know you care about being professional. I get that. You're not just pissed at me though. You're defensive."

"No, I'm not." *Ah!* What am I, a toddler?

"You like him, don't you?" she fishes, even though her face says she already knows the answer.

I don't reply. I don't even look at her. The tiny flower growing up from the crack in the concrete to the side of my right foot has suddenly become the most fascinating thing in the whole world.

Cassie laughs. "Well, don't be a fool. He was looking at you like you were the leading lady in his romantic comedy and I was the D-lister cast as your friend."

I try to ignore the leap my heart takes into the air at the

thought. I look up and shake my head. I've already gone through this a million times in my head; it always ends with the same outcome. "It doesn't matter. Samantha would fire me."

Cassie's eyes soften kindly, and she reaches for the keys in her purse. I know she's angling for the last words here, and I'm willing to give them to her. I'm exhausted from trying to bail water out of my sinking ship.

"You've done everything for the girls these past five years. You've been the best mom in the world to them, at the expense of yourself. This job isn't meant to last forever. Maybe this is your opportunity to actually do something for you."

I don't have a single good response. I just stand there watching Cassie get into her car and pull away.

When I get back to the kitchen table, Elliott has disappeared. I'd be grateful for the moment to myself, except he's on a constant loop in my head anyway. The lonely silence makes a sad soundtrack for the images of his wide smile that are burned into my brain.

At least I have my project to distract me. I pull open my laptop and double tap on the trackpad. The light flickers on and displays my login screen, and then it skips into a smooth black nothing.

No. No no no no no no no. No!

My whole academic career is on this laptop, and my Dropbox filled up at the end of last semester. I forgot to move some older files to my portable hard drive, and it hasn't synced since the spring term ended.

I lost my entire competition entry. The whole thing. More than a dozen hours of work are gone.

I quickly run through my options. It's due tomorrow. There's no way I can recreate it, even if I left for home right now. I don't have any of the programs I need installed on my mom's computer. The school computer lab is only open until 2am.

SON OF A MOTHER LOVING TWATWAFFLE.

I slam my fist against the table and pain radiates immediately from my pinky all the way up to my elbow. I pinch my eyes and lips shut to keep my scream from bursting out.

"Everything okay?" Elliott asks softly. I jump, oh, about ten feet into the air with a squeak. So much for keeping quiet. I didn't hear him come in, but considering he's by the back stairwell on the other side of the kitchen, he probably came from upstairs.

"My computer just died." My throat starts to close up and the edges sear into each other.

"Your project?" I know in those two simple words Elliott's asking if I backed it up. I can't utter the words. I lost it. It's gone. The burning in my throat sends warm pools to my eyes, and I can't hold it in. I collapse my arms on the table and deep sobs crash like waves breaking onto hard rock.

I can hear Elliott slide into the chair next to me, and I feel his arm reach across my back. My body craves the comfort. I lean over and bury myself into his chest before my brain can even approve. He's the life preserver that's been tossed in my direction, and I'm not going to keep treading water without it.

I don't know how long we sit there, but when I pull way

there's a giant wet mark on his shoulder, punctuated by flecks of brown mascara.

"I'm sorry." I nod toward the stain.

Elliott just lifts his shoulders with a smile. "Hazard of the job."

"What job is that?" I ask curiously.

"Making sure you're okay."

My breath catches, and if I hadn't just expelled nearly half my body mass in water onto his shirt, I would probably lose it. Aside from my mom—who I know from personal experience signed an invisible, ironclad document to protect me—no one has ever cared about taking care of me. That's my job, and it feels entirely foreign to be on the receiving end.

"We're going to fix this," Elliott says as he squeezes my shoulder. I know immediately that he will do anything to make this right, and suddenly everything does feel like it's going to be okay. I don't know how yet, but I do know I don't have to figure it out alone.

Chapter 25

Zoey

Apparently, fixing this problem is as easy as a drive into downtown Chapel Hill—or so Elliott says. Right now, I'll take any glimmer of hope he gives me.

This glimmer comes in the form of "knowing a guy."

After Samantha comes home, Elliott and I get into my car and head off to Franklin Street. He leads me to a tiny strip mall off a side street and I pull into a parking spot in front of an electronics store with more neon signs than there are glow sticks at a rave.

I have no idea how much this is going to set me back, but I'll pay practically anything to recover this project. It's my chance to break into the industry.

I grab my laptop, pulling it close to my chest like my little baby that broke its leg. There's a college girl sitting behind the counter at the back of the store and I immediately hope this isn't the "guy" Elliott was talking about. *He said* guy, *right?* I can't remember.

I get closer to the counter and I swear I can practically see the foam padding of the pushup bra she's wearing beneath her low cut V-neck shirt.

Please don't be his person. Please.

She doesn't look up even as I step up to the counter right in front of her. I hear Elliott step up behind me. I desperately want to pull him close to me—both to feel his skin crackle like fireworks against my own and to claim him as mine.

I need to smack myself. He's not mine. He can't be mine.

Elliott shifts to the right of me and steps up to the counter. Miss V-neck perks up immediately and flashes him a seductive smile.

Now I just want to smack her.

"Hey, man!" A voice jolts me out of my aggressive fantasy and I turn to the right. Tucked behind a pile of old monitors, a disheveled head peeks out with a full smile.

"Hey Duncan!" Elliott reaches out his fist and bumps it with the guy sitting in the corner. "This is Zoey, and we need a serious favor."

"Anything, man! You saved my ass in econ. What can I do for ya?" Duncan pushes his chair back from his desk and listens as Elliott explains the situation.

I can see Miss V-neck leaning over, trying to get Elliott's attention, but he's focused on asking Duncan a million questions. I get lost in computer translation about three words in, and I just let Elliott and Duncan work their magic. V-neck leaves for the back room a minute later and Elliott doesn't even notice. I want to run a victory lap around the store, but I settle for a goofy grin that reaches up toward my ears.

125

An hour later, everything is off my computer safely and, as Duncan assures me, in one recoverable piece. It's on a portable hard drive. Something with the graphics card had failed and my computer played dead. Duncan couldn't fix it immediately, but he said he can work his magic and have it back to me in a couple days.

All I have to do now is wake up early to hit up the computer lab with the files from the drive and finalize my submission.

So, this is what it feels like to be taken care of? To have someone in your corner to grip your shoulders and tell you you're going to be okay when the brute in the ring hits one dead on.

I just keep hearing Cassie's voice over and over, like a well-worn piece of paper that's been folded and unfolded a hundred times: *Do something for you.*

For the first time in a long time, I really want to.

Chapter 26

Elliott

It's just after Stewart's bedtime when I get back home. I head into the main house to grab something to eat, and I run into Sam walking out of the kitchen with papers tucked under her arm and a glass of water in her hand. She looks up at me over the thick black-rimmed glasses she wears at night.

"How was your *errand?*" she asks with emphasis on the ambiguous excuse I made earlier for skipping out before dinner. I didn't say anything about Zoey's broken computer, and I'm definitely not going to now.

"Fine. How was dinner?" I counter. The trick to Sam, I've learned, is to not let her rile you. The moment you show even a hint of getting worked up, she wedges her way in and makes it worse.

"Fine." She stares at me for a second, like she's trying to decide whether to engage or not. So, I just focus on pulling out some leftovers. When I close the fridge door, she's gone.

I roll my shoulders back and try to release some of the tension. The closer I get to Zoey, the more careful I have to be.

Sam is a hawk, and I know she's watching this situation for just a hint of movement in the wrong direction.

I would stay away, but every moment I spend with Zoey makes me want ten thousand more. She makes me want to step up and become a real adult—to be someone who is worth her time and not just some loser crashing in his sister's pool house.

I sit down with my pork fried rice and pull out my phone. I've spent the last five days doing nothing but look at every single job listing I'm remotely qualified for, everything from consulting to working as a line chef at a greasy spoon. Okay, so maybe I'm not entirely qualified for that last one, but I'm handy with a frying pan and good under pressure. Plus, I look surprisingly handsome in white. Line chefs wear white, right?

The fact is I've pressed send on probably fifty applications in the area and exactly zero back in Cali. I feel more at home living here in my crazy sister's pool house than I ever did in the land of venture capital dreams and overpriced apartments with twenty roommates and three rooms.

It's funny how much I wanted to escape North Carolina when I was graduating college. I wanted to run as far away as possible from my parents' expectations and the same old bars I'd gone to since I was tall enough to pull off twenty-one. It felt bland and unappealing to stay. I bought a one-way ticket to the Bay and hopped around from startup to startup until I had an idea that felt strong enough to peddle for funding.

It was exhilarating, and lonely. The highs were few and the lows were dark clouds that never seemed to completely blow over.

Since I've been back, I've appreciated the broken in t-shirt feel of home. The color may be faded, but years of wear have made it so thin and soft it feels like just another layer of skin. It's a part of you.

And North Carolina has Zoey. It sounds crazy, but I don't want to move away from this. From her. There's something there, and I want to spend all the time in the world trying to explore what that is.

When her computer broke tonight, I knew I had to do everything I could to fix it—not because I wanted to be some hero, but because I wanted to help her, to make her life a little easier. She makes my life easier every time she's around. I avoided her when I first moved in, and every time we would run into each other, it was the highlight of my day. That's not something you step away from, even if the circumstances are less than ideal.

I don't know if Zoey agrees with me about that part yet, but I made progress tonight. When we were done at the electronics store, her entire vibe was different. She was quicker to smile, and she didn't try to keep six feet of distance between us like she has been. I know it wasn't just because she was happy her computer and all her work was going to be brought back from the edge of a black hole where computer files go to die.

No. She likes me. I know it, and I think she's finally opening up to the idea that we might be worth the risk.

Chapter 27

Zoey

I'm practically flying with energy as I pull into the MacCallister house. It's been one of those amazing mornings where the world feels like it's moving in slow motion while you're moving at warp speed. I've already been to the computer lab, turned in my competition submission, had a morning dance party with the twins, and consumed about eighty billion ounces of coffee.

I'm due for a caffeine crash at some point today, but that's a future problem for future Zoey.

All I can think about is walking through the front door and seeing that amazing superhero of a man I really want to hug but am most definitely not going to actually hug. Even though I want to. I totally shouldn't. I would, but I can't. But I would.

That's probably the caffeine talking, with backup vocals by my lady parts.

Yup. I should probably set down this large drip coffee as soon as I get inside.

I open the front door and make my way back to the kitchen

where the smell of bacon hits me like a déjà vu two-by-four.

Elliott is making breakfast again, and this time, he's whistling. I have to admit, I hadn't pegged him as a whistler. Somehow it's innocently charming and panty dropping all at the same time. He catches my eye and I melt on impact. God, it feels good to stop avoiding him.

He winks at me, and any resolve against diving in simply evaporates. I mean, please. The man is cooking breakfast and winking at me like we're both in on a big secret.

Or should I say secrets? Cause they're currently in an epic elbowing battle for who's the biggest in this room.

Elliott and I both know Samantha can't know about us. Even if it's only a light flirtation, that's one flirt too many in her book.

But, I have a sneaking suspicion the whole I-have-twins secret is the big gun here.

Every time I think about this whole situation with that filter, it feels like I just slammed a cheap beer. My stomach revolts, and I seriously question my life choices. I know it's going to come back and haunt me, and the taste is going to be even more vile coming up than it is going down.

I push it aside, like a stupid tipsy novice who throws potential consequences out the window, ignoring that they're going to have to open the door and face them in the morning.

Please. Did I mention he's making bacon? All the best life choices involve bacon. My inner tipsy voice agrees.

I'm tempted to wink back at him, but we're not alone. This already feels reckless. I don't want to add stupidity to that bonfire.

Samantha walks in and stares at Elliott while Stewart walks right over to grab a plate and wait patiently for his breakfast, like a sixty-year-old in a three-year-old's body.

I can't figure out if Samantha's contemplating actually eating something that doesn't fall within the guidelines of her very regimented list of acceptable foods to eat or if she's playing detective in this situation.

She turns to me and I realize I haven't pulled oxygen since she stepped into the room. I quickly will my lungs back into action, which results in a sort of quick, raspy cough. She tilts her head to the side, but then like a switch, she snaps out of investigator mode and right into litigator pro.

"I've had a last minute meeting come up with our top client in Charlotte. I need to head straight there after work for a dinner meeting and then a joint work session in the morning with our team out there. I understand this is last minute, but I will pay you double for your time. In cash."

I try to quickly do the math, but I don't have to multiply fifteen by two and then by however many hours an overnight trip would entail to know it's too good to pass up.

I look at Elliott, and he isn't even trying to hide his massive grin while he stands just out of Samantha's peripheral vision. All of a sudden, his wink takes on a whole new context.

My stomach jolts into motion, quickly climbing up a cool hundred stories and dangling its toes out over the edge.

Samantha catches my glance at Elliott, and he covers his grin just in time for her to turn around to him.

"If you're unavailable, I'm going to have to call a backup sitter. After the stunt Elliott pulled last night, I don't trust him to watch Stewart."

Elliott's grin returns like a Cheshire cat. "It was an accident. I was just singing out loud."

I hold in a smile, but I can't stop my curiosity. "What did he do?"

Samantha turns back to me, her lips pressed into a straight, unhappy line. "He was rapping, and Stewart picked up a few choice words."

"A little Macklemore and Ryan Lewis isn't going to hurt him."

"Well, I'm certainly not going to find out what you'd do with twenty-four hours." Samantha shoots him a stern glance and then turns back to me with a rare smile. "I've made Elliott promise he will stay out of your way."

Elliott nods his head, but the glimmer in his eyes shows he has little regard for his agreement. He probably crossed his fingers behind his back while he offered up a pinky swear. I have four-year-olds; I'm well-versed in the methods of sneakiness. You have to ask to see both hands out front while you get a promise. Apparently, Samantha is better at written documents than verbal agreements.

Before I even think it through, I hear myself saying, "Sure, I think I can stay. Just let me make a quick phone call."

Samantha agrees, and I pull my phone out of my purse and walk into the front office to quickly talk to my mom.

When I walk back into the kitchen two minutes later, I have confirmation that I can stay.

I don't know if I'm going to say yes or no until I walk in and see Elliott's face. He's handing a plate of pancakes and bacon over to Stewart, and I'm overwhelmed by the desire to indulge myself in spending time with the first man I've come across in the past four years that looks at me like I am a whole person instead of one divided by three—a piece for myself and one for each of the pieces that came from me.

"I can stay."

Samantha looks relieved, but I only catch it out of necessity that I show more interest in her reaction; I'm engaging the peripheral line of my vision to gauge the reaction I really care about.

When I see Elliott give the air the tiniest little jab of a punch, my stomach reaches one foot over the edge and then jumps straight off.

Chapter 28

Zoey

Before I can even blink, it's Stewart's bedtime. The day feels like it passed by in a matter of seconds.

We went to the park and ran around until the three of us couldn't even move the tiniest fiber of a muscle. It was lunchtime when we got home, and then Elliott had to race out for an appointment. He didn't give me any details, only a smoldering smile and a vague comment about "adulting." There was napping, coloring, more food, and now I'm lying here reading a bedtime story with Stewart tucked under my arm.

I turn the last page and then close the book. "Okay, Stewart, it's time for lights out. I'm going to be sleeping just down the hall in the guest room if you need me tonight." I kiss his sweet forehead, knowing I'm going to miss this quirky little old soul when he goes to preschool full time this fall. This could be my last sleepover for all I know.

I have my girls, but Stewart has become my little man. It breaks my heart to think that Samantha would probably file a restraining order if I ask to still see him. Do nannies even do that? I fell into this by chance, and it feels like I've been scrambling the whole time to figure out the rules and boundaries of the nanny-family dynamic.

I resolve to nudge Samantha about still calling me for babysitting.

Stewart looks up at me as he curls into my side, stretching his arms around my waist. "I love you, Zoey. I had the best day with you and Uncle Elliott. You're my favorites." He releases my waist and tucks in under his big cushy blue comforter.

I close my eyes, trying to capture the feeling of his squeeze as the rest of me melts into a big puddle of joy. "I love you too, Stewart. Goodnight, buddy." I kiss his forehead and dim the nightlight before tiptoeing out of his room.

I just barely contain a gasp when I notice Elliott leaning against the wall opposite the door. His arms are crossed, but his demeanor is anything but closed off. His eyes are soft as they meet mine, and I melt for an altogether different reason.

"He's got good taste in favorites." Elliott smiles and pushes off the wall. "I grabbed his monitor from the counter. Want to go enjoy the sunset out by the pool?"

I swallow. This feels like walking out on the high diving board for the first time—exhilarating and really fucking scary. You're desperately trying not to look down at how far away the water is, and for a second you wonder if you could get away with climbing back down the ladder.

There's that tiny little voice in your ear screaming, *Don't be a wimp, just jump! Count to ten and DO IT!*

"Sure," I finally offer. He nods in happy agreement that I've let the voice in my head persuade me into it and we make our way down the stairs.

I follow Elliott as he takes a detour into the kitchen to open the fridge. "I grabbed some Coronas on my way back home today. Want one?"

I've got one toe over the edge of the diving board when I remember I'm not here to have fun. Maybe climbing up to jump off the high board really was a bad idea.

"I probably shouldn't. It's my job to watch Stewart." I have responsibilities. I can't be stupid. Only fools jump.

"I'm not trying to get us drunk. Parents have one beer all the time after their kids go to bed," Elliott reasons. He looks at me and sees my struggle. "It's okay if you don't, I just don't think it's a problem if you want to have one beer. You're not a delinquent for kicking up your feet and relaxing with me tonight."

He's right. I know he's right. I've had enough wine after the girls go to bed to fill the barrels of a small winery.

It just feels like my life has been defined by my mistakes—or rather, my singular, alcohol-induced mistake. I've been so scared to misstep, I keep my life confined within the tight boundaries of what's acceptable.

Having a beer with the brother of my employer while I'm being paid to watch her sleeping son is a gray area. I've tried so hard to avoid the muddy line between good and bad choices.

Cassie's voice surfaces from the cacophony of arguments in my head. *Do something for you.*

137

I take a deep breath and reach out for the beer. "Let's do this."

Elliott laughs. "Are we having a drink out by the pool or going to a rave?" I blush and he nudges my shoulder playfully. "You're so serious about this, like deciding whether or not drinking one beer was a matter of national importance. I promise, the Corona is not that good."

I take a sip and swallow dramatically. "Seems pretty damn good to me."

Elliott swallows, even though he hasn't even lifted his beer to his mouth. "I knew I liked you."

I dip my head at his statement, unable to meet his eyes when my heart is pounding so loudly I swear it has its own PA system. Even though it wasn't meant to be some grand declaration, it still feels like he just handed me a note back in class with the yes box checked.

This whole situation is so incredibly foreign. Cassie used to joke that I had my "light" turned off after the girls were born— that I actively gave off a vibe that implied I'd rather eat gravel than talk to a member of the opposite sex.

She was right.

No one gives you a manual on how to navigate motherhood, and they absolutely don't have a version for single mothers.

I don't know what it's like to love the father of your children. I don't even know what it's like to climb under the covers at night after a long day full of crushed Cheerios and unrelenting tantrums and relax against another warm body who loves me just as much as my girls.

I tucked those desires away into a dark closet in the farthest corner of my brain and tossed the key into my hideously disorganized mental junk drawer.

I know I'm risking unlocking that dark closet and flashing a bright light in. It's likely that by leaving those desires on their own for so many years, they've grown exponentially and morphed into a demanding horde of beasts with very strong preferences.

I'm starting to think it isn't strength that keeps me from facing my desires. It's fear.

Chapter 29

Zoey

"So what happens after summer's over?" Elliott's voice jars me back to reality, and I nearly choke on my beer as I sit down on a pool chair. "I mean, Stewart is going to full-time preschool, right? And you mentioned finishing up your degree soon."

Aha, right. We're talking about normal day-to-day life, not if I'm considering whether or not I plan on dating him when this job is done.

Cause I'm totally not thinking about that. All the time.

Liar liar pants on fire.

What am I doing after this all changes? "Well, I'll find a job in graphic design. I'll feel totally lost without seeing Stewart all the time, so I should probably try to figure out if your sister would take out a restraining order if I showed up to visit him."

Elliott chuckles deeply, and I decide he has one of my favorite laughs. I've always thought you have to love someone's laugh in order to really like them. Well, check and check.

"I wouldn't put it past her, but I'll sneak you in for visits." He winks.

"So, you're planning on sticking around?" I've wondered this exact question to myself over and over. Part of me hopes he plans on moving away again so this casual summer interest doesn't have a chance of making it even two inches off the ground. That's the part that doesn't know how to be a mom and a girlfriend at the same time.

The part that wants him to stick around is growing day by day.

"Definitely," he answers. "North Carolina is home, and if I'm honest, I was trying to prove something by moving to California."

He's staying, and my skin tingles in happy anticipation. It's no secret now which part of me is winning the turf war.

"What were you trying to prove?" I wonder aloud.

Elliott touches his mouth to the rim of the bottle in thought. "That I could break the rules and succeed. I wanted to prove I didn't need to be a published professor or a partner at a law firm in order to be successful."

"Did your parents want you to follow in their footsteps?" I'm curious how Samantha and Elliott are so different.

"They pushed me toward it. My dad's a law professor at Duke; I don't know if you knew that. He took a sabbatical this past spring and they're traveling while he works on writing yet another textbook. My mom was with Sam and me full time, and it was always the unspoken assumption that we'd both go into law. I mean, we were raised by one of the greatest law professors to grace our country's law schools." Elliott's voice is shaded by

141

several degrees of sarcasm. "Why wouldn't we when we were debating contracts and tort at the dinner table every night?"

"But you didn't."

"Nope."

"Why not?" I think I can guess why, but I'm finding I want to know what goes on inside Elliott's head just as much as I want to keep listening to the deep, rich tone of his voice.

"Because I'm the youngest child. Because I don't actually believe the world needs more lawyers. Because I think there are more interesting problems in the world than whose argument is better or what loophole gets you what you want."

I'm suddenly overwhelmed with gratitude for my mother and her unwavering encouragement to pursue whatever dreams called to me, and I'm even more attracted to Elliott for following his own interests despite not having the kind of unconditional support I did.

"Were your parents upset that you pursued a business degree?"

"I think they were just glad I didn't major in philosophy, which I seriously considered for a while. I just liked my business classes more. I knew I was pursuing philosophy to piss off my dad more than anything else."

"You'd think as a law professor, he'd appreciate philosophy," I muse.

"A philosophy class, yes. A whole major dedicated to it with no intention of going to law school? Hell no. It wasn't that much different in the end when I moved out to the Bay and ended up in the startup scene. He was still pretty pissed."

"I don't get it. I'd be insanely proud if my kid moved across the country to be in tech—even more so if they started their own company like you did."

"That's because you were born after the sixties. Kids who grew up in the eighties and beyond know the tech industry is solid, but to the old schoolers like my dad, it's just another temporary bubble that's going to pop. It's not going to help that I didn't succeed."

"They don't know yet?"

"No, and I haven't really been dying to call them up in Antigua or Poland or whatever country they're in now to tell them I'm back home and my company is over."

He shrugs, but his shoulders don't melt back down all the way. There's still a knotted ball of unpleasant feeling lodged deep under the skin. I don't want to press too hard, even if that's the best way to unravel it, so I only apply soft pressure. "What was your company? What did you do?"

Elliott smiles, but it doesn't even make it up to his cheeks. "We provided online courses to teach people—especially young adults—real world skills, like for understanding personal finances or how to write a killer resume or what to ask when you're looking for your first apartment."

"Damn, that sounds useful."

"It is, it's just nearly impossible to monetize and even harder to create kickass content on a tight budget. We could have used your design expertise."

"There are a million and a half graphic designers out there. I didn't exactly choose a field where I'd be invaluable." I've kicked myself over and over, but in my delirious, new mama state after the girls were born, I wanted something I knew I could excel in and have a reasonable chance of finding a job in. I'd loved my art classes, so graphic design seemed to be the best fit.

"I saw your work on your laptop the other day. You're talented at what you do, Zoey."

"You're just saying that because you like me." The words rush out in a brazen blur, naturally deflecting the compliment. Apparently, half a beer is enough to evaporate my filter.

"I do like you." Elliott catches my eyes and holds the gaze. "But I also think you're good at what you do, and you can certainly handle difficult personalities. I think you would have been an amazing colleague."

"Are you saying you're a *difficult personality?*" I use air quotes as I tease him.

"I have a little bit of MacCallister in me still."

"Which means...?" I can tell by the twinkle in his eye he's steering us in a direction he clearly wants to go. The trouble is, I'm definitely okay being led there.

Elliott leans toward me. "Which means being stubborn about getting what I want."

I drag my bottom lip against my teeth before taking a long drink from my Corona. "And what do you want?"

Elliott swings his legs over the side of the pool lounger and stares straight at me with a wicked grin on his face. God, people shouldn't be allowed to have teeth that white and straight. It's a blinding hazard.

"I want to go skinny dipping." My breath catches, and the oxygen left in my lungs feels like it's on fire. "With you," he adds, just in case I thought this was a one-man show.

Before I can even think through where I stand in relation to the yes or no line of this situation, Elliott pulls his shirt over his head and flings it to the side.

I thought his teeth were blinding, but I am not prepared for the perfection of what hides beneath his shirt all day.

I'm gawking. I know I am gawking, and there is absolutely nothing I can do about it. I am like a teenager who just discovered how to turn off safe search on Google. There's no turning back now.

I want to take a picture of him and hang it up in my closet so I can fangirl over him every single day.

"We haven't even gotten to the best part." Elliott's grin grows even wider and he stands up and unbuttons his shorts. He turns toward the pool, but even in that brief moment, I know he has a lot to offer beyond cut abs and perfectly sculpted pecs.

A lot.

And then he starts to peel off his boxer briefs. I don't have to see his face to know he is enjoying every single cocky second of this. He's pushing my boundaries, and he's loving it. He knows it, and I know it.

His briefs are off for a solid three seconds before he dives into the deep end of the pool. I wish reality had a slow-mo feature, because I would have enjoyed every single stunning frame.

My lips are completely dry. I'm parched, and yet I'm sweating like I'm trying to cheat on the SATs. This is not a test. I could stare at him until I went blind, and even with the image seared into my brain, it still wouldn't be enough.

It takes me four long gulps to down the rest of my beer. I still don't know what I'm going to do, and I'm trying to draw out my decision. The only problem with my stalling tactic is that there is an entirely naked man—the most attractive naked man I've ever seen in my life—who just surfaced at the edge of the pool…which means my mind is completely blank. There are no useful powers of thought going on right now. I'm still breathing; that's about as much as I can handle.

"The water's really nice." Elliott makes it sound like this is just a stroll along the beach as he fans his arms back and forth on the surface of the water.

I get up from my chair. I'm either going to say goodnight and beg out of this whole situation like an awkward jellyfish, or I'm going to walk over, take off all of my clothes, and dive in.

I take one step closer to the pool.

"I'll turn around if you want," Elliott offers.

I have a sneaking suspicion from the way he's looking at me that he's already undressing me with his eyes.

I swallow and then finally admit, "I've never actually skinny dipped before." Elliott guffaws like a cartoon character at my confession. Coming from a currently naked Adonis, it's both unexpected and endearing.

"I don't even know how you've lived in North Carolina your whole life and never gone skinny dipping, but I'm pretty sure now that you've admitted it, you have to jump in this pool with me."

It is sort of strange that I've never done this before, an odd combination of the right opportunity never arising and not seeking out the thrill of doing something on the wild side—even if it is pretty innocuous when it comes down to it. It just always felt so foolish. I've always counted how many things could go wrong from point A to point B instead of allowing myself to get caught up in the moment.

The thing is…I want to. I can feel it in the way my feet are pulling toward the edge of the water. My body is overriding my short-circuiting brain.

I want to take off all my clothes and see what happens; that is the only thought that flits through my brain as I begin to peel off my t-shirt.

I swear I see Elliott momentarily lick his bottom lip, but he turns around so quickly I can't decide if I just imagined it or not.

I push off my shorts and underwear and toss them to the side before slipping my fingers underneath my bra hook and snapping it open in one fluid motion. I toss it into the tiny pile to my left and take a deep breath, pulling in both the courage and the oxygen that propel me forward into the water.

The water rushes over my skin quickly, and yet I swear I can feel it conquer each inch in sweet slow motion. It reaches my toes and then I arc my body back up toward the surface. When I open

147

my eyes, I see Elliott facing me with his lower lip pulled underneath his top teeth. I was right; I did see him lick his lips.

It hits me: he thinks I'm sexy. He went birthday suit first because he wanted to see me in mine, and the I'll-get-naked-first strategy is a winner. Clearly.

I feel femininely powerful in my skin, and now I completely understand why Cassie told me to go for it. Feeling attractive is one of the most amazing feelings in the universe.

"God, you're the most beautiful woman I've ever seen, and that's at least twenty reasons down on the list of things I like about you," Elliott whispers as he slowly wades over to me.

I let the compliment sink in, relishing it rather than trying to deflect it.

Elliott is right in front of me before I can respond, which is fortunate because any semblance of coherent thought has left me completely. The water is warm, but my skin is covered in goose bumps.

"Do you know what I want to do right now?"

A tiny gasp is all my brain offers in response.

Elliott reaches out, tucks a piece of hair behind my ear, and closes the gap between us until we're inches apart. "I want to kiss you."

He doesn't wait for a response before leaning in and pressing his lips to mine. It's soft at first. I take a step toward him until our bodies are pressed against one another, and I can feel the hard ridges of his body pressed against mine. I move my arms up his shoulders and wrap them around his neck, taking us both over the edge of soft and deep into the pool of desire that's swirling between us.

Elliott meets my pressure and reaches down to grab my legs, wrapping them around his waist and then working his hands around to the small of my back. We're so close, I'm not even sure water can fit between our bodies any more.

He reaches his tongue out to graze my top lip and then pulls it back, nipping my bottom lip with his teeth. He pulls back and gives me a smile heavy with need, and I know my face is a mirror to his.

My body is screaming for him. I am aware of every cell in my body and each one is alive with a sizzling electricity I've never felt before. It's intoxicating and overwhelming. My brain can't make sense of anything beyond the moment we're in.

Elliott leans in to kiss the tiny shell of space between my jaw and my earlobe. Every single electric impulse currently flooding my body travels to that exact sliver of space beneath his lips and explodes. I pull in a skipping gasp of air.

His lips travel along the ridge of my ear and then he whispers, "You're so fucking sexy, I've never wanted anything more in my life than you in this moment."

I close my eyes and bite my lip with a smile. I feel exactly the same way.

A loud cry breaks the moment and my eyes fly open.

Stewart.

A flood of logic and guilt sweeps through my thoughts, crashing against the walls of the moment.

What the hell am I doing? Am I fucking crazy? I'm naked in a pool with my boss's brother while I'm supposed to be watching her son. This is insane! I have to get out of here.

I unlock my legs and push away from Elliott. "I'm sorry. I have to go."

I swim across the pool toward my clothes. The monitor is silent again, but I don't dare turn around. I can't face Elliott. I don't trust myself to say no to him, and if I don't walk away now, I might make a huge mistake.

Chapter 30

Elliott

I don't know what came over me. I was all about taking it slow, having a nice beer out by the water. Maybe it was the beer, or maybe it was just my own impatience, but without thinking it through, I stripped down and jumped in the pool. I knew I was calling Zoey's bluff. Was she going to walk away or jump in?

She jumped, and we got swept up in the moment. I know why she ran; doesn't mean I don't hate it. This situation is a cluster fuck.

I walk over to the enclosed outdoor shower and step in to rinse off the chlorine. I close my eyes and step under the shower head, trying to let the water drown out the competing voices in my head. It doesn't do much to help. I want to pat myself on the back and smack myself at the same time.

That kiss. The feeling of Zoey's body wrapped around mine. It was better than I could have ever imagined.

But when reality broke in, she ran.

I can't blame her. Her ass is on the line. My sister would fire her in a heartbeat. Hell, she'd probably kick me out of the pool house just to grind some salt into the wound.

And if Stewart saw us? I don't even want to think about it. Sam would go all mother-of-dragons on us. Total and complete destruction. I know it, and Zoey knows it.

I took two steps forward tonight and then lost a whole mile. There's no way Zoey is going to come within six feet of me now. That really makes me want to smack myself. Repeatedly.

I turn off the water and grab a towel and my pile of clothes, reaching into the pocket of my shorts and pulling out my phone.

I shoot a text off to Brandon.

What are you doing tomorrow?

No plans yet.

Good. I'm coming over. Let's beer and cable.

Sounds good.

I know Zoey's going to avoid me whether I'm around or not; I might as well make it easier.

Brandon's been bugging me about some business idea he wants to run by me anyway. After today, I'm going to need all the distraction I can get. It's going to be damn near impossible to forget the feeling of Zoey wrapped around me like a vine curling around a tree. It's a dangerous relationship, but once that vine is coiled, there's no way to untangle it without harming both parties.

I lay down on top of the sheets and close my eyes to replay the visual of Zoey starting to peel off her clothes. At least that can't be scrubbed from my memory. I'm going to rewind that five seconds over and over until I wear it down to sepia tones and faded corners.

I was a fool for rushing it, but I'll never regret the jump.

Chapter 31

Zoey

When I finally make it back to my house the next afternoon, I'm exhausted.

When I open the side door, the house is eerily quiet. For a second, I think everybody is gone, but then I see the outline of a tiny body sitting on the couch in the living room. When I step inside, I see Louisa's arms crossed and tears streaming down her face. I'm about to ask what's wrong when the door to the girls' bedroom shuts and Cassie comes walking toward me in her waitress uniform. My exhaustion looks like a full night's sleep next to the look of complete energy drain on my sister's face.

Damn, it's one of those days.

She points to the kitchen and I follow her through the doorway.

"The girls have been at each other's throats all day. This is their fourth timeout in the last hour." Cassie's voice is a crisp whisper, but even in her low tone, I can hear the frustration.

My guilt kicks it up a notch. My girls needed me today. My sister needed me. Where was I? At the zoo with a perfectly well-behaved boy while trying to avoid the man I made out with last night.

This is why there is no doing things for yourself in motherhood. There's some cosmic karma dump that puts you back in your place the moment you take time for yourself.

"Mom has a massive migraine," Cassie continues. "I finally got her to take some medicine and lie down."

Our mom has life-halting headaches from time to time. She's not good at stopping herself, even though the tiniest bit of light or sound is excruciatingly painful. I'm immensely grateful Cassie was here.

"I've got to run to my shift at the restaurant. I'm on until closing. I'm sorry, there's nothing in the fridge for dinner."

"It's okay." I wave it off; a food shortage is the least of our problems. "I'll run to the store. Go to work, and don't worry about us."

Cassie nods, grabbing her purse off the counter and heading out the door to mom's car.

Just as she's through the doorway, my gratitude catches up to the problem-solving mode my brain shifted into. "And Cassie, thank you. I know it isn't easy, and I really, really appreciate your help."

Cassie gives me a huge grin. "That's what sisters are for."

Sisters are the best. I don't know what I would do without Cassie.

My heart breaks a little whenever my girls fight. I wish they could see how incredibly important they are to each other, but I can't skip straight to the heart of the lesson. I can only give them a strong foundation and then some time and space to figure it out for themselves. Heaven knows Cassie and I had our own battles growing up, and we made it out okay. I have to believe Phoebe and Louisa will do the same.

I make my way to the girls' bedroom to get Phoebe. When the three of us are all back in the living room, I switch into serious mom mode.

"Okay, your Aunt Cassie told me it's been a rough day. Grandma's in her room and her head really hurts. We need to get out of the house and give her some time to feel better. I don't want to know what happened between you two today, but I do want both of you to sit in the back seat quietly until you're ready to give each other a hug and apologize."

I can practically feel the steam pouring out from Louisa. She is fiercely stubborn. We're probably going to sit in the car in the parking lot of the store for a while before she caves.

Phoebe is standing facing me with her arms crossed in a perfect mirror of her sister's. They are so similar, it's comical. I know better than to laugh, but I wish I could at least take a picture.

"You ready to go?"

Both girls nod silently and we head out to the car.

Chapter 32

Zoey

I set the stopwatch on my phone when we pull into the Kroger to appease my own curiosity about how long we'll sit in the car—five minutes and forty-five seconds.

I guessed six minutes and thirty seconds. I hadn't accounted for how quickly the car would heat up, even with all the windows down. There's no breeze in the air and my hair is clinging to the back of my neck like wet Saran wrap from July's wet heat.

I catch Phoebe starting to shift in her seat in the rearview mirror, and I look up to see her make her way over to Louisa, wrapping her arms around her sister's shoulders. "I'm sorry for taking your Lego set and finishing it," she mumbles hesitantly, unsure of Louisa's reaction.

Louisa sighs. Nothing breaks down her stubborn demeanor faster than love from her sister. My heart melts when she embraces her sister back. "I'm sorry I ripped all the hair out of your favorite Barbie and flushed it down the toilet."

Ouch. It really was an epic battle today.

"I love you."

"I love you too."

Louisa leans forward, resting her arms on the center console. "Can we go get food now, Mom? I'm hungry."

I'm happy to oblige, and we all head into the store.

I'm not embarrassed to admit that I will happily indulge in a little carb therapy to combat a case of the seriously no-good, very bad day.

So, as we're rounding the last corner, our cart is stocked full of fried chicken from the hot-and-ready section, Oreos, chips, and a Caesar salad mix to give us some croutons with a side of veggies in one guilt-reducing shot.

We're standing in front of the discounted wines while I try to recall if we have any at home and the girls debate the merits of the newest flavors of Oreos they saw on the shelves; it's serious business all around.

I almost don't hear my name at first. It goes in one ear but then out the other while I continue to sort out my wine dilemma.

Someone calls out Zoey again, and I look up just as I realize I know that voice.

I turn around and see the face of someone who just saw me naked. He's still twenty feet away, but I can tell by the way his lips sneak up to one side he's thinking about exactly that. I take a deep breath and try desperately to avoid doing the same.

It's harder than I thought it would be. Even in shorts and a t-shirt, I can still see the broad expanse of his chest, and my breath stops when I remember what it felt like to be wrapped up in his arms.

I don't have time for reliving fantasies. Elliott continues toward me with a case of beer under his arm and a guy to his left that I don't recognize. The look on his friend's face shows he certainly seems to know who I am.

Shit. Shit, shit, shit, shit, shitty shit.

My mind shuffles through exit strategies, but each one becomes increasingly unhelpful as Elliott gets closer.

I can see him take note of Phoebe and Louisa, and I wonder for a second if their blonde hair and greenish blue eyes are a dead giveaway that we're related.

When he gets to our cart, his smile has faded and his brows are hunched down with confusion. I can see in his eyes that he's quickly trying to process the variables of this situation.

I don't even bother trying to process what's about to happen. I'm so underwater I'm not even going to bother raising my arms toward the surface. I'm not even remotely close anyway.

"I didn't realize you had other nanny gigs," he says. He's trying to be nice, and I want to laugh. I've been avoiding a moment like this with Samantha for years. It became second nature after a while, and now, we're here. It may not be Samantha, but considering I was just wrapped around this man in my birthday suit less than twenty-four hours ago…it's probably the worst case version on crack.

Phoebe and Louisa have stopped talking, and they're alternating between looking at me and looking at Elliott. I suddenly wish I had asked them to be quiet and go along with whatever I say, but my mom brain is well aware that I can't lie in front of them. They pick up on what I do more than any advice I give about telling the truth and being brave. Even if I could explain it away, it's still a bad example.

I swallow, knowing what's coming next as Louisa turns to me and opens her mouth to speak. "Mom, who's that?"

Elliott's eyebrows reach high and his mouth drops open as he processes the information bomb that just exploded in front of him.

I don't wait for him to finish trying to understand what's happening. "This is Stewart's uncle."

Elliott clears his throat, his manners overriding whatever is going on in his brain. He reaches his hand out to Louisa and then Phoebe. "Hi, I'm Elliott."

"This is Louisa and Phoebe." I take a breath and add, "My daughters."

Oh hey, elephant. You're looking awfully neon pink today.

"I didn't realize…" he starts, but struggles to piece together any words to follow.

"Yeah, Samantha doesn't know. I would appreciate if you would let me be the one to tell her."

"Right." Elliott nods absentmindedly, still working through the trillion thoughts strewn across this whole situation.

"Well, I'll let you get back to it." I gesture to his beer, eager to extract both of us from this disastrous run-in.

"Yeah, I came up this way to hang out with Brandon." Elliott motions to the guy standing next to him and shifting awkwardly from foot to foot while trying to pretend he's keenly interested in the Cupcake brand's new wine display. "We needed some beer, so we came here. I didn't know this was by where you lived."

"Yup," I reply brightly. *Get me out of here.* "We needed to get food for dinner, and we're pretty hungry, so we're going to race off. See you later."

I start pushing the cart away and the girls miraculously follow me without uttering a single word. I don't care that I basically just walked away from the conversation; I couldn't handle another second.

No one says a word until we're walking through the automatic sliding door out to the parking lot.

Phoebe looks up at me when I stop the cart to wait for a car to pass.

"Mom, that was serious-awkward-turtle-times-infinity back there," she says while making that little hand gesture with one hand over the other, thumbs paddling. I don't even know where she picked that up, but something tells me Cassie has been filling them in on all sorts of random pop culture.

She's right. It was awkward-turtle-times-infinity, and her spot-on perception makes me smile. At least it's something to distract me from the fact that my life just walked itself off a cliff.

Chapter 33

Elliott

Brandon and I get to his house without saying more than five words to each other. It's not abnormal for us, but I appreciate the silence nonetheless. I can't quite wrap my head around what just happened. *Zoey has daughters.*

I'm trying to piece through every moment, every situation. It's like I've been experiencing this summer in shades of black and white, and someone just switched it over to the full color wheel. I'm trying to rerun our history and paint it in with Technicolor.

Zoey's hesitation makes even more sense now. The stakes are higher for her. She isn't just talking about some job to support herself. She's a mom.

It shifts things into focus, but it still feels like I got hit by a speeding train.

Zoey's a mom.

There are a million thoughts buzzing around like a beehive in my head. They're bumping into each other, flying in and out. I can't seem to make any one of them be still long enough for me to focus on it.

Why was she hiding this? Was she scared of how I'd react? Is the father involved?

I open up the case of beer, grab one, pop the tab open, and drink half a can without so much as blinking. When I set it down, I see Brandon smirking at me from across the room.

"If that's how the day's going to go, tomorrow's going to be one hell of a morning."

"Can you blame me? I just found out she's a mom."

"And?" Brandon leans forward in his chair like he's challenging me to work through this.

"That's a hell of a big bomb to drop on someone."

"You wanna know what I think?" He stands up and walks toward me, grabbing a beer out of the case. He opens it and makes a point to take a long sip.

I just raise my eyebrows. Brandon is not one to keep his opinions to himself, so my answer is a moot point.

"My dad didn't do jack shit to raise me except send along paychecks. My mom did all the work. So, when I say you better know what you want out of this, I mean it. Don't dick around with her. I guarantee she's already dealt with more than you could handle in your lifetime. Don't stick around unless you're going to make her life easier."

I remember the rumors in grade school about Brandon's dad moving out to live with his secretary. We knew it was scandalous, but none of us really understood why. I never thought of him growing up with just one parent. We always hung out at his mom's house, but his dad was always in the background; I

163

assumed he was still part of the picture. I guess a blurred figure in the distance doesn't make it a two-parent family.

Still, I feel like Brandon is trying to tell me solving differential equations is as easy as understanding algebra. "It's not that simple, dude."

"Well then, let me ask you this, are you in it just for a hookup?"

It doesn't take me even a split second to answer. "Hell no."

"Do you have that feeling? That can't get enough of her, want to be around her, have to make it happen sort of feeling?"

I stop and think about how I've felt from the moment she opened the door to the moment she dove into the pool and wrapped her legs around me. I've wanted to be around her every single moment in between. I've pushed that feeling to the side, trying to avoid the complications of our particular situation. That feeling hasn't left; it's just underneath the rubble.

I don't have to answer. Brandon sees the look on my face and nods. "She's still the same person, she just has more weight on her shoulders than you realized."

He's right, but it doesn't make any of this less surprising. I pull the can of beer back up and take the second half in three satisfying gulps. I need to process this. I know I still feel the same way about her, but Brandon is right. I need to know for sure that I'm going to make her life easier.

Chapter 34

Zoey

When Cassie finally gets home in the wee hours of the morning, I've practically worn a tread line across the floor of the living room. I tried lying down in bed, but my brain was screaming too loud for me to even try to fall asleep.

I rolled around for a while, and then I got up to get a glass of wine and then try again, but the wine only brought a more neurotic level of crazy into the mix. So, I started walking, half hoping to tire myself out, half trying to see if physical motion would calm my brain down.

Yup. That didn't work.

Cassie jumps with a small squeak when she catches me out of the corner of her eye. I stop for a split second, long enough for her to realize it's just me, and then I keep going, one foot in front of the other.

It's like those first few weeks of motherhood when the girls had no concept of day and night and the only thing that soothed them was constant motion—except at that point, I had no concept of what life would look like even two weeks in the future.

Now I know my life is going to look like a bad afterschool special.

Girl gets pregnant at eighteen. Girl gets job as nanny. Girl lies about being a mom. Girl falls for brother of employer. Girl gets caught in lie. Girl gets fired. Girl loses biggest reference from the past two plus years of employment. Girl can't get job. Girl ends up being that loser who works crappy jobs all her life, lives with her mom, and never catches a break ever again.

It's 3am. Logic says I'm being a tiny bit dramatic, but logic got shoved out about two hours ago. It's in the trashcan outside where its tiny cries for reason and sanity are wasted.

I catch Cassie's eyes and she looks at me with both sweet understanding and *Girl, you are going batshit crazy*, which is pretty much exactly what I would expect. She motions for me to follow her out to the back porch where our voices won't travel to the still sane humans who are actually getting sleep in our house.

She picks up the open bottle of wine on our way through the kitchen. I almost tell her not to bother but then think better of it. I don't know how I can talk about this without simultaneously IVing my anxiety with wine.

We haven't even sat down when Cassie uncorks the discussion. "Okay, spill."

I tell her everything. From Elliott prying my morals loose with bacon to running into him at the grocery store, it all comes rushing out.

When I'm finally done, I reach for the wine and perch the thick glass rim against my lips. "I can't stop thinking about how good it felt—to be wanted, to feel desire, to act on it—and every time I go down that path, I turn my brain into a boxing ring, because look where it got me." I take a long drink and then finally look over at Cassie.

Her fingers are resting against her mouth while she thinks. My hand starts to ache, and I look down to see I have a death grip on the wine. I'm so nervous for what she's going to say. I trust her more than I trust my own brain right now.

"He didn't say he was going to tell Samantha."

"No."

"He didn't even imply that he would, or that he was thinking about it."

"No. He just seemed pretty shocked."

"Right." Cassie says it like it's a definitive answer, but I don't see how it's anything remotely in my favor.

"Yeah, but he knows, and she's family."

"You have this whole situation linked together in your brain like a chain of events that have been set into motion and isn't going to stop until all the cars have passed through, but it's not a linear situation. It's a bunch of tiny clusters. Some of the clusters overlap and some of them don't." She tries to use her hands to aid her explanation, but it doesn't help my comprehension in the slightest.

"You lost me at the train bit. I need plain English minus fancy metaphors."

Cassie turns her entire body to me, swinging her legs around so they hang over the side of the chair, like it's imperative to make sure she communicates this correctly. "You made out with

Elliott, and you both are obviously attracted to one another. You didn't get caught, but it's technically against the rules."

"Pretty sure it's one hundred percent, without a doubt, against the rules."

"Whatever." Cassie waves me off like a fly buzzing around her logic. "That's one set of events right there, and it's separate. You like each other. Full stop."

I open my mouth to argue, but she gives me a look—the look that says, *I'll pull all the hair out of all your Barbie and flush it down the toilet.*

I shut my mouth.

"You freaked out and ran away, and I get it. I'm pretty sure Elliott can understand it too. You two are in a tricky situation."

I nod, grudgingly. *Fine, that part might be true. Proceed, sister logic. Proceed.*

"Then you ran into him at the store, and he found out you were the mother of two adorable little girls."

"Two little girls that neither he nor his sister know anything about." My eyes are wide as if opening them to their full capacity is crucial to getting the point across. Cassie just shrugs. "This is not a nonchalant shrug sort of situation. It's a really big deal. I could get fired for this."

"I'm not saying it's not a big deal, but I think your greatest fears and Elliott's greatest fears are two very different things."

The thought stops the train that's been running nonstop in my head with a loud screeching halt. Cassie sees the pause and keeps going, ready to drop even more knowledge bombs.

"You're afraid of getting fired. You're probably afraid of making one wrong move and sending your life into a downward spiral you can't recover from. I one hundred percent think you're being way too hard on yourself, but we'll get to that. The thing is, Elliott's not freaking out about that. If I had to guess, he's wigging out over if you have a secret husband or some baby daddy back home. He's worried this might be more complicated than he had originally anticipated. He's freaking out that he might have to court three women, two of which are prone to very loud, very irrational bouts of emotions. He's not worrying about what he's going to tell his sister."

"You don't know that for sure!" I argue indignantly; it's the only part of her otherwise completely reasonable logic I can attack.

"Is he male?"

"Yes."

"Does he tell his sister everything, including being attracted to her super hot nanny?"

I can only respond to her with a death stare.

"He's not going to tell her, and certainly not before sorting things out with you first."

"I don't agree with you." I can't, no matter what sensible thoughts I add to my head; they're pitifully quiet compared to the litany of crazy.

"Doesn't make me any less right."

"I'm going to get fired. I know it."

"We'll figure it out if you do."

169

"Aha! You think she's going to find out." I point at her like some CSI detective in the last five minutes of the show. Caught ya!

"No, you could get fired because you sneeze the wrong way, or because Samantha opens up the photos folder on your phone to look for a picture of Stewart and puts two and two together. If you don't finish this job to the very last day, it'll be okay. You'll find another job. The bigger issue isn't your job. It's your love life."

That statement earns two full chugs of wine. I would rather focus on my disastrous on-the-job decisions than dive deep into my love issues.

"You're not going to do irreparable harm to your life or the girls' lives if you fall in love. I actually think you stand to do more harm if you keep love at arm's length. Show them what it means to be loved and to give love. Show them that being vulnerable is important. And dear god, if you have to, show that you can heal if you get your heart broken. Don't be a perfect mom who never takes risks. Be an imperfect mom who shows them the immense beauty there is in simply being human."

I'm stunned. Even if my brain was working properly—which at nearly 4am, it absolutely is not—I don't think I'd know what to say.

Cassie stands up and puts a firm hand on my shoulder. "I'm crazy tired, and the girls are going to be up soon. Get some sleep, OK?"

She walks through the porch door, and I'm left trying to make sense of this jumble.

I'm still irrationally worried I may not have a job on Monday, but I finally realize it might be the least of my problems.

Chapter 35

Zoey

I get a text on Sunday night from Samantha asking me to come in fifteen minutes early, and I'm a nervous wreck all the way up to turning the keys in my car's ignition on Monday morning. Then I realize I can't change her mind, and something about that thought is freeing.

When I pull through the wrought iron gate of the MacCallister's subdivision, I'm shocked to see Elliott standing there on the sidewalk. He waves at me and makes his way toward the passenger seat.

He gets in and smiles. My stomach does a flip. I'm about to walk the plank, and he still makes me feel giddy inside—how's that for confusing?

"Can you pull over into the clubhouse lot for a few minutes?"

I don't press the gas, confused by his request. "But I'm supposed to meet your sister."

"Yeah…that was me. I filched her phone last night, texted you, waited for you to reply, and then deleted the text," he offers first. Then he adds, "I didn't know if you'd show up if I asked you." His devious smile is outlined with traces of worry.

Damn, one point for Cassie. His worries are very different than my worries.

I drive us over to the lot and park, but I leave my seatbelt on and start playing with the peeling leather on the bottom right of the steering wheel like it's the most interesting thing I've ever seen.

"I think I should be perfectly honest with you," he starts, and my heart sinks like it's been thrown into the deep ocean with the weight of reality chained to it. "I'm really attracted to you. I like you, and that isn't something I say lightly. I haven't felt this way about someone in a long time…maybe ever."

My heart starts to break off some of the heavy chains pulling it down.

"But Saturday threw me for a loop." His eyebrows are pinched in the center, like he's been creasing them over and over again in heavy thought. "I've been missing a huge piece of who you are, and that really woke me up to the realization that I don't know you very well."

Oh no. Here it is—the fear I tuck away in the dark corners of my mind, careful not to acknowledge it exists, because if I bring it out into the light, then maybe it'll become painfully real.

I don't deserve love.

I close my eyes and brace myself for the impact.

"I want to get to know you," Elliott says so softly I almost wonder if I imagined it. My eyes fling open, but I can't look at him, in case this isn't real. "I don't just want to walk around

173

dreaming up ways to flirt with you or to jump into pools with you. I want to take you out to dinner. I want to spend an afternoon at the park with you. I want to kiss you knowing we're both really interested in this being more than some forbidden flirtation."

I finally turn to look at Elliott. His eyes are hopeful, and I've never wanted to kiss him more than I do in this moment. "Are you trying to ask me out?"

He laughs and reaches out to brush his thumb against my cheek. I want to lean into this feeling forever. "Yes. Zoey, may I take you out to dinner?"

I bite my lower lip before I can say yes. My worry still stands. I could get fired for this. Dating my boss's brother is without a doubt on the do-not-attempt-under-any-circumstances list.

Elliott exhales deliberately, but he doesn't move his hand away from my face. If anything, he puts all his energy into the connection. "It doesn't have to be tomorrow. You're not going to work for Samantha forever. Say yes to a date the night after your last day."

I want to say yes, but it feels too good to be true. "You realize I'm a mom to two four-and-a-half-year-old girls, right?" I feel obliged to point out the elephant, just in case he missed the blinking hot pink light-up shoes it's wearing.

He laughs in his deep baritone. "Yes. That part was extraordinarily obvious at the grocery store."

I still feel like he's missing it. "I got pregnant when I was eighteen years old. I am the one-in-twenty teenage girls who got pregnant. I'm on the wrong end of the statistic."

"I'm impressed that you're pulling stats out of your back pocket." He's still smiling, but I keep waiting for him to let what I'm saying sink in and for his smile to fade.

"When you're on bed rest at eight months pregnant and all your friends are either at college or partying whenever they're not working some crappy nine to five job, you spend a lot of time on the Internet."

"You're trying to scare me away like you're damaged goods, and you need to know it's not going to work."

"You say that now, but what happens when you take me out and you realize that beyond graphic design, the only thing I do is take care of kids. It's ninety percent of what I talk about. I'm not interesting dating material. I'm boring, and I'm a mess more often than not." I feel as if I've flipped on the flood lights and I'm waiting for his eyes to adjust to seeing what's been hiding in the darkness.

Elliott is as relaxed as ever. All I see is kindness in his eyes. "I don't think you're giving yourself enough credit. I've been intrigued by you since the moment you answered the door. You don't have to be some Instagram mashup of a traveling yoga teacher do-gooder who speaks ten languages and learns how to craft beer in their spare time. You're more interesting in your own imperfect way than anyone else who tries to imitate fascinating by cramming their life full of photo-worthy moments."

"Well, then maybe you're crazy."

175

"Maybe I am. I dare you to find out."

I take a deep breath and look at the car clock. It's almost been fifteen minutes. If we keep talking, I'll be late. "I need to go."

"You didn't say yes," he points out.

"I didn't say no, either."

Elliott doesn't like it but sees that the conversation is at an impasse, and he reaches for the door handle. Just as it clicks open, he turns to me, locking eyes. "I'm going to do everything in my power to get you to say yes. I want to go out with you, Zoey Porter, because contrary to what you may think, you are the most fascinating woman I've ever met."

He swings the door open and gets out, shutting it behind him and pushing off into a jog. The weight of the conversation leaves me stunned. I drove here today sure I was about to be fired, but instead the man I am wildly attracted to asked me out despite discovering what would make most men run the other way.

I'm flattered and confused and excited and scared.

A woman passes in front of the car on her way to the clubhouse. She waves at me even though I can tell by the confused look on her face she doesn't quite understand who I am and why my shitty car is parked in the lot. It's enough to pull me out of my thoughts and get me on my way to the house. I'm about to be late, and if motherhood has taught me anything, it's that some things really do come before your need to sit and process your feelings.

Chapter 36

Elliott

I spend the whole day trying to act as if everything is normal. I took a risk by stealing Sam's phone last night to get Zoey to come in early, but it felt even scarier to get in that car today and ask her out. I genuinely didn't know if she would say yes or not. I'm not the biggest fan of asking questions I don't already know the answer to—a trait I can thank good old dad for.

After my conversation with Brandon, I spent the rest of the weekend thinking about what I wanted, and there wasn't a single second when Zoey wasn't the answer to that question. I don't know if I can make her life easier, but I sure as hell want to try.

For now, that means trying to act like a normal human being around her, not one who has been pulled into her orbit and wants to unwind into the circular rhythm. It's a hard balance to act interested but not overeager.

Fortunately, Stewart is the best distraction I could have asked for. We spent the whole day building an epic Lego set and playing outside in the pool.

Now, I'm standing over a pot of what will soon be meatballs

and marinara sauce—my mom's recipe. It's a killer dish, passed down from the Italian side of her family. I don't even think it's ever been written down; it's just something that's been taught from generation to generation.

Zoey walks downstairs with Stewart after getting him out of his wet swim gear. She inhales the scent of the onions and garlic and her eyes go wide. Making a meal is an innocent enough endeavor, but I can tell by the way she's looking at me, she's thinking there is nothing sexier than a man in the kitchen. I'm not stupid. Cooking has always been my no-fail hook, and it's reeling in the big one this time.

"Stewart, why don't we work on being Uncle Elliott's helpers tonight?" she asks without taking her eyes off me. *This was such a good idea.*

"Okay!" Stewart says brightly.

"I'm helpless with anything but stirring and pouring," she says to me with her lips pulled into a dramatic grimace. It's so goofy and adorable. It's a good thing Stewart's here to keep things kid friendly.

I start walking Stewart through the steps of our family recipe, asking him to help with some of the easy parts from time to time. I selfishly keep Zoey in my direct line of vision, asking her to stir the noodles. The burner is off—they're not even cooking yet; if she notices, she certainly doesn't say anything. She sits up on the counter, next to the stove, and turns the wooden spoon from time to time.

I would give anything to know what's going on in her head,

but I'm guessing from the happily distant look in her eyes it's not Stewart friendly. Good. I want her to think about us and what we could be, because I think it could be pretty fucking spectacular.

Hell, it is going to be fucking spectacular. I'm going to figure out how to make this happen, no matter how long it takes.

Chapter 37

Zoey

Elliott knows his way around a kitchen. The confidence and ease with which he tosses ingredients together while having a conversation with Stewart about what he's doing is so incredibly attractive.

I can't get that kiss in the pool out of my head. He was so sure of himself—just like he is now. I could sink into him and know he was there to hold us both up for a while. I've never had that before.

I've been holding myself up for so long now, and it gets tiring. My family props me up, but it's not quite the same. I desperately want to lean in and let go for a moment. I've never found someone I've felt comfortable enough to do that with.

Until now.

The realization hits me like a train speeding along at three hundred miles per hour. I feel comfortable with Elliott.

Yes, he makes me nervous, but in a fluttering stomach, oh-my-goodness-what's-going-to-happen-next sort of way. It's about exciting possibility, not about fear of the unknown.

A voice in my head whispers, *I shouldn't say no any more*. I'm finally inclined to agree.

"Dinner's almost ready," Elliott announces. "Stewart, why don't you grab the plates on the counter and set the table for us?"

Stewart agrees with a quick nod of his head and a giant smile. He's happy to help the uncle he admires so much and he scurries off to his task.

Elliott watches him walk into the separate dining room and then he's over to me in two steps. I'm perched on the counter and he slips right in between my knees, grabbing ahold of my thighs. I feel like I could levitate, as if my skin has grown millions of tiny, happily flapping wings.

He looks me in the eyes and lowers his voice to a barely audible whisper. "I've kept it PG all day, but I want you to know having you this close to me all day has been driving me crazy. I want you, and I want you to know that. I want you to say yes."

I almost forget where we are. It's just the two of us and the desire that feels like it's taking the last steps toward a summit. I nearly bend down to press my lips to his.

I hear Stewart's little feet padding back into the kitchen and Elliott breaks his connection. Stewart bounces in just as Elliott steps away, and a great big smile spreads on his face.

"Mom!"

Time slows to an army crawl through thick mud.

Elliott turns on his heel and we both look over to see Samantha standing in the doorway with the fiercest straight face I've ever seen. I don't know how much she saw, but just a glance at our faces would be enough evidence to damn us.

Even Elliott is stunned into silence. Stewart is the only one of us that seems to be functioning normally. He runs over to Samantha.

"Mom! We're having 'ghetti and meatballs!"

Samantha gives him a small smile and lets Stewart lead her through the kitchen to the dining room.

My brain kicks back into gear and immediately jumps into flight mode. "I have to go."

I hop off the counter and I'm nearly to the kitchen doorway when Elliott finally breaks his silence. "Zoey," he whispers softly, cautiously. I turn around and he mouths with a barely audible whisper, "It'll be okay."

I want to believe him, but I know I just watched the lit match finally hit the fuse I've entangled so carelessly around my life.

It's everything I can do to make it out to my car and buckle in. By the time I've pulled my keys out, the adrenaline has caught up to me and I'm shaking so badly I have to use two hands to get the key in the ignition.

That was it. All my worrying, and in one single moment, it all came true.

Chapter 38

Zoey

I wake the next morning to the sound of rain tapping on my window. The sun hasn't started its ascent up the horizon, but I can already feel the gray of the day ahead. I can't tell if it's originating in the clouds outside or if it's seeping out from my bones and spreading to the air around me.

I listen for the girls, but all I hear is the hum of the air conditioning that never seems to take a break during these oppressively hot July days. I grab my phone and make my way out to the kitchen to start a pot of coffee. I have no idea what the day will hold, but it will be twenty times worse without caffeine.

I see the light of my phone, bright against the shadows of the dimly lit kitchen. I already know who it is before I see it.

Sick day. No need to come in.

It's an ambiguous omen, and I almost rethink my mug of warm coffee. Maybe I should just go back to bed—except there's no way I can get back to sleep now, and I have two bundles of energy who'll wake up any minute.

I sit down at the table and stare out at the big maple tree in our side yard. I remember scaring my mom half to death by climbing nearly to the top, with Cassie always just a branch below in the adventure.

I was so brave back then. You think you're invincible until you're not. I got that wakeup call from the end of an entirely different kind of stick.

Motherhood makes you wake up with a different sort of bravery, one where you're completely aware of all of the risks and pitfalls in life and you have to climb out of bed and face them with daring vulnerability.

I liked climbing to the tops of trees better. I'd rather live like I could never fall than walk along a completely normal street and worry that every pothole is a risk for breaking a leg, contracting gangrene, and never being able to walk again.

Noise begins to travel out from the bedrooms and little feet rush toward the kitchen first.

"Morning, Mama!" Phoebe and Louisa cry out in unison. I get a quick hug before one reaches for the cereal and milk and the other grabs the bowls and spoons.

"You two are moving quickly this morning." They don't really have a slow speed, and it's usually a game of make-believe here and a quick sing-a-long there before we make it to breakfast.

"Aunt Cassie is taking us to school today!" Phoebe exclaims happily, and Louisa nods while gobbling up her Honey Nut O's.

As if on command, Cassie emerges with a big eye rub. She worked a late shift and usually isn't awake until the hours hit double digits.

She reaches for the coffee pot and a mug. "My friend is teaching at this theater summer camp for kids, and she said if I came to help corral, I could bring the girls with me."

Louisa takes a break from inhaling her cereal to add in an ultra sophisticated tone, "We're learning the art of the-a-ter, Mama."

"Yeah, we're gonna be actresses!" Phoebe chimes in.

Cassie sits across from me, eyes barely open.

"I can take them," I offer. "Samantha is taking a sick day today."

She takes a long satisfying sip from her mug. "Eh, I want to go. Get to see my backup plan."

Cassie always jokes that half of all theater majors end up teaching. I think it's her way of making herself feel better about majoring in something most people would consider frivolous compared to biology, but I don't doubt for a second that she's going to be one of the few who do truly succeed.

"Are you sure? I could go for the first few hours at least, while you get more sleep." I want to add that I really need the mental distraction, but we've both had too little coffee to get into the source of that desire.

"It's cool. This coffee will kick in and I'll be great. I'm a college kid, remember? This is like a full night's sleep for me."

I realize I'm not going to win this one without divulging the entirety of my current situation. So, I focus on getting the girls ready to get out the door on time—a feat that requires total concentration and a lot of steering.

185

By the time all three of them are in the car and ready to go, my mom is up and has poured her own cup of coffee; it's the Porter drink of choice. She sits down at the table and I pull out the seat across from her.

"Cassie mentioned you don't have to go in today."

"Nope, I have the day off." I stop myself from adding that I may have every day off from now on. "I tried to convince Cassie to swap places with me, but she really wanted to go."

My mom nods. "She loves spending time with the girls. I think she's trying to cram in half a year's worth of visits into two months before she has to go back to LA."

I've been mentally avoiding that thought. I wish I had my sister around all the time. Boys may come and go, but Cassie will always be my better half. I'd keep her close if I could, but there's nothing better than seeing her happily pursuing her dreams. I'll take that over having her stuck in the narrow arena of our hometown any day.

"We could have a mother-daughter day. It hasn't been just the two of us in a very long time." My mom smiles.

I suddenly want nothing more than the comfort of cuddling up next to my mom and passing the day away in a mindless haze. "Netflix binge?" I suggest.

"How early do you think we can get pizza delivered?" She winks at me deviously.

I love my mother and her total commitment to the art of relaxing. She has worked so hard for so long as a teacher, a single mother, and now a secondary caregiver. When she gets a break, she doesn't try to cram in as many to-dos as she can. No, she sits down and chills the fuck out. The woman knows how to take a break, and I love it.

Chapter 39

Zoey

Six episodes of *Gilmore Girls* and a large meat lovers pizza later, we finally get up and scope out what we can whip up with the ingredients in the pantry. Mug cakes are a serious contender, but we're currently researching if half a box of Chex is enough to do muddy buddies justice.

My mom is measuring out exactly how many cups of cereal we have. "So, what's really going on, dear?" She doesn't even look up, as if she's merely asking about the weather.

I practically drop the jar of peanut butter I'm holding. I didn't think I was letting on that there was anything out of the ordinary going on. Sometimes I forget I got my awesome mama superpower of knowing exactly what's going on without anyone having to say it from the woman standing three feet away.

I consider lying, but I know that's just pushing the conversation off to a later date. My mom doesn't push us to talk to her immediately any more, but that doesn't mean she gives up. She uses the slow water-drop method instead now, using time to break us down instead of force.

I'm not quite ready, so I ask curiously, "How do you know something's up?"

"You kept sighing every time a love interest showed up on screen. Besides, you've been on edge for a few weeks. I had a sneaking suspicion when Cassie mentioned Samantha's younger brother had moved in with her. You never brought it up. It seems like you've been avoiding talking about it."

Nothing gets past her. I release my shoulders helplessly. The knots are still there, but I'm not going to keep squeezing them like I'm trying to wrap rubber bands around a fist of loose marbles any more. I spill about my attraction and how I've tried to avoid it. I leave out the pool incident, but I mention yesterday's close call. My mom finishes stirring together the ingredients and then leads us to the kitchen table.

She sits quietly for a second, her hands wrapped around an oversized mug of muddy buddies. We're definitely going to eat the whole bowl, but we like to start with the false premise of moderation.

"Do you want my advice?" she finally asks.

"Yes. Desperately."

"Jobs come and go, but the chance for love is not something that's as simple as sending resumes out for."

I look at her with shock. I honestly didn't know what she would say. I knew it would be supportive—as a teacher, my mom mastered the art of encouragement—but we don't talk about love. It's always been the ultimate taboo in this house. We could talk about sex—we got a very informative and embarrassing talk when our periods started—but romantic love? We didn't touch it with a ten-foot pole. My mom never mentioned it, and somehow Cassie and I decided we would avoid it too. It's only been recently that my sister and I have even opened up to each other about it.

In high school, talking about a crush was something saved for sleepovers at someone else's house. Boys were deemed nice or cute or smart at our house, but once we were away from these four walls, those adjectives expanded into "totally dateable," "hookup material," and "heartbreak waiting to happen."

Geez, Cassie and I didn't even have our prom dates pick us up. I later realized my mom was silently bummed about losing out on the photo op; we were just so used to dodging the topic, we took everything even remotely similar off the table.

My face must read like an open book because my mom laughs. "I don't know when you girls got it into your heads that I'm some loveless puritan, but it's not true. In fact, I think love is one of the most important things we can surround ourselves with. We need the love of family and friends as well as romantic partners."

"But you never talked about it!" I throw my hands up. This is all news to me.

My mom sighs out the weight of something that must have been sitting heavy on her mind for years. "Do you remember when you were in the sixth grade—you were eleven and Cassie was nine—and I brought a man to the house? Or rather, he stopped by before taking me out to dinner. I had hired that babysitter you girls loved."

I know exactly what babysitter she's talking about—the one who would sit and color with me for hours. I can't remember any man ever stepping foot in the house, besides the select few who were hired to do some sort of repair. I shake my head no.

"That shouldn't surprise me, but it does. I guess it was only a traumatic evening for me." My mom laughs and closes her eyes, massaging the bridge of her nose. The irony isn't lost on her.

"What happened?"

"You girls didn't know this, but he and I had been quietly seeing each other for months. His name was Rex, and he was a really lovely man. I was finally ready to introduce him to you both, and so we engineered a very low key introduction. I can't remember all the specifics—I've blocked it out—but you two were miserable. You were rude and disrespectful. I was embarrassed. I knew it was the product of it being us three girls for so long. Seeing me with a man was a jarring experience. It took a long time for me to get over it, and by the time I did, it had just become a habit to keep that part of my life private."

My mind is blown. "You've been going on dates this whole time?"

She smiles. "Book club is only once a month."

"You've been going on dates three out of every four weeks and we never knew?"

"Sometimes I just go to a restaurant and have dinner by myself and read, but yes, I frequently have dates."

"With Rex?" I silently wonder if I have some almost stepdad and don't even know it.

191

"Oh heavens no. He was gone shortly after that disaster of an introduction."

I feel a deep pang of guilt. "We really screwed it up then." We didn't know what we were doing, and we didn't think about the consequences of our actions. We don't even remember it.

"No," Mom answers with a comforting smile. "He was a lovely man, but he was pushing for marriage. I didn't want that. I still don't. I enjoy love, and I think companionship is an important part of life, but I don't want to deal with the legal hoops of divorce ever again, and I don't need a piece of paper to believe someone is committed to me."

The way my mom says it sounds eerily like she is committed to someone. "Do you have a boyfriend?"

"Yes." She blushes. I've never seen this woman turn that crimson before from anything that wasn't a hot flash. She didn't even flush when she had to explain what the boys were talking about when they were curious about if girls were okay with the back door. I couldn't poop without feeling fifty shades of embarrassed for months after that educational conversation.

I want to know everything about this *yes* of hers and the questions pour out of me. "Who? How long? What's his name? What's he like?"

She nods, knowing she just opened Pandora's box. "His name is Bruce. He's a retired Air Force general, and we've been together for about five years now."

"How did we not know about this?" I'm flabbergasted. This is such a huge part of her life, and we've been oblivious.

"I got really good at keeping it secret. Bruce has a grown son, and he was never in any rush to tell him either. His wife died a couple years before we met, and he didn't particularly want to share that he was falling in love again with anyone who might still be grieving the loss. We've been on the same page, and so it's been a lovely thing to have just between the two of us."

"So, it's serious then?"

"Very much so."

I don't know what to say. My mom has been in love for longer than I've had the girls, and I never knew. I can understand her reasoning, particularly with Bruce also wanting to keep it on the down low. I feel a twinge of frustration at being kept in the dark, but it's quickly replaced by the pleasant happiness that someone out there loves my mom and she loves them back.

She reaches out for my hand and I reach back, feeling the soft weight of her love.

"You never know if you're making the right decisions as a parent. You know that firsthand. I didn't intend to outlaw all mentions of love in our house, but by the time I realized it was an unspoken rule, you both were teenagers. It's not exactly an easy topic to talk about when there are a million new thoughts and feelings and experiences happening. So, I left it alone. I argued with myself that maybe you and Cassie wanted to keep that part of your life private. I'm sure I was projecting that desire, and we all ended up keeping it to ourselves. I don't know that it was the right thing in retrospect. I want you two to have love and to value the pursuit of it." Tears begin to pool in her eyes. "It's the most important thing."

I reach out and cover our two clasped hands with my other hand. "It's okay, Mom. You didn't screw up."

"Well, whatever I did couldn't have been too awful because I have two of the most wonderful daughters and the best grandchildren I could have ever dreamed of." She wipes her eyes with her free hand and then places it on top of mine with a squeeze. "You'll find another job, and I know enough about both of our finances to know that if we need to pinch for a while, we'll be okay. Pursue love. Even the inkling of it is more important than a job that couldn't matter less in your pursuit of a career in graphic design. I might tell you to step cautiously if you were at some design firm, to really know if this was something worth the risk, but you've worked for that grumpy woman for long enough. I say go for it."

My phone vibrates from the table in the family room, and I know this is it. I look at the screen and see *Samantha MacCallister* in bold white script at the top.

Here goes nothing.

Chapter 40

Zoey

My mom squeezes my hand and I get up, quickly rushing to catch the call. I tap accept and press the phone to my ear.

"Hello. Zoey?" Samantha's voice crisply breaks through the digital airwaves.

"Yes, this is Zoey."

"Good. I called to inform you that I will no longer be requiring your services."

You're fired would have been good enough. Either way, it doesn't sting as badly as I thought it would. It's more like the tiny punch of a flu shot than stepping on a Lego in the middle of the night.

"Okay." It's the only response I have. I'm not going to beg her to reconsider; I don't think she would anyway, so it would just be wasting both our time.

"I've noticed your behavior has become unacceptable." She pauses for me to argue, but I can't really disagree with her. She's not wrong. I am—was her employee, and I wasn't exactly one hundred percent professional on the job.

"I don't know why I didn't do this before. You were meant to be a temporary fix." It's a purposeful dig, and I swear I feel the fire in her breath as she says it.

I have to bite my inner cheek to keep my mouth shut. She's just trying to push buttons now, and that makes me want to punch her in the ovaries. Before her brother came along, I was the best goddamn nanny she'd ever had.

She continues, "But then I got a phone call from a neighbor who saw you and Elliott together in your car at the clubhouse. When I came home and saw you, well…I don't know how long this has been going on under my nose, but know that you will never have a job as a nanny again."

I don't bother mentioning that after this job, I don't plan on being a nanny again. I don't know that she even knows I'm getting a degree in graphic design. She certainly never bothered to ask beyond knowing I was going to classes when I first started working for her. I'm not going to tell her now that I am a semester and a half away from graduating just so she can try to blackball me in that industry too.

I won't have a reference for this job, but I'll figure that out later. There's nothing I can do to change it right now. "I understand."

"That's it? That's all you have to say?" Her words are full of sharp edges, but I just let them fall to the floor.

"I'm sorry to have put you and especially Stewart in this situation. I hope you find a good replacement soon."

"I've already employed the services of a firm that specializes in matching nannies to employers. I'm just glad Stewart didn't seem to catch on to this unacceptable behavior."

"Me too." I close my eyes at the thought; it would have been a disaster on so many levels.

"You admit it then."

Damn. I shouldn't have said anything. She's just baiting me. "I'm sorry, Samantha. Is there anything else I can help you with?"

I can almost hear her stunned expression at my polite but curt response.

"No. That's all." Click.

Well, it happened. It really happened, and I'm going to be okay. I'm shaking with leftover nerves, but that'll pass.

I hear Cassie and the girls walk in the door, and my mom whispers something about me being on the phone. I walk back out to the kitchen and the girls rush over to envelop me in a hug. My mom mouths, "So?" and Cassie knows enough to be curious.

I mouth back, "Fired." The girls don't need to know this yet. Both my mom and sister give me sympathetic looks, but they're quickly masked as soon as the girls turn around.

Right now, all I need to do is be a mom. I'll figure out the rest later.

Chapter 41

Elliott

The last twenty-four hours have been like sitting down in the right classroom but the wrong class. Everything looks the same, but the material is completely different. I know Sam is pissed. She's walking around like she's going to go all Dexter on the first person who looks at her the wrong way. If I see her carrying around large sheets of plastic, I'm screwed.

I ran into her when I was in the kitchen grabbing breakfast, and she informed me that she would be taking a sick day. I wanted to ask what was going on with Zoey, but I'm not stupid enough to point the hunter toward new prey. So, I just asked if she needed any help. Judging by the glare I got, I'm assuming she's got it covered.

I escaped to the pool house and have been holed up here all day. Thank god I brought enough food with me to last a week. It's almost dinnertime and I still haven't worked up enough nerve to go in and face whatever's waiting for me inside. Disownment. Firing squad. Slow and painful dismemberment. Whatever it is, I'm scared it's ten times worse for Zoey.

I want to call her or at least text her, but I don't know what to say. *Oh hey, sorry I probably cost you your job. How about I take you out to dinner now?*

This wasn't how I saw this going down. I want to kick myself. It's my fault. I walked over to her and put her in a compromising position because I'm impatient. That's what it comes down to. She probably thinks I'm a total dick. This is exactly what she was trying to avoid, and I handed it to her in a haphazardly wrapped package with a squished bow. There wasn't even anything good inside, just some flirtatious intentions and a serious case of I-can't-keep-my-damn-hands-to-myself.

I've been trying to work on applying for more jobs. I had an interview the day before last when Zoey was here. I said it was an appointment because I didn't want to jinx it, which is good because the interview itself was a joke. A friend of a friend recommended me, so I thought it was legit. Turns out it was a manager training scheme. I wanted to tell the guy he couldn't pay me enough to show up for 90 hours a week to "learn the business" when it was clear they just want to run you to the ground on an abysmal salary with no overtime. Instead, I just ground my teeth and smiled. As much as I hated it, I'm not in a position to burn bridges—even if I wanted to tell him where he could put his leadership building: right back where the bullshit train came from.

My phone vibrates for the first time all day and my heart skips a beat. *Zoey?*

When I flip it over to check the screen, I see Brandon's name

199

across the top instead. *Yeah, okay. Good, but not great.* "Hey dude, what's up?" I answer.

"Remember that idea I ran by you last week?" Brandon doesn't even wait to hear my response, and I don't have to see him to hear that's he's practically hitting the roof with excitement. "I ran it by my dad, who ran it by some of his friends, and I'm sitting with a few million of angel investment in a business account."

Whoa. I didn't even understand half the shit he was talking about, but it doesn't take a PhD to understand that he intends to revolutionize the medical industry. The fact that he not only got his dad's seal of approval but serious starting cash that quickly… Brandon is onto something.

"I want you to come be the CEO. I'm horrible at that side of things. I need a pretty face to come distract everyone while we hit them out of the park with our business acumen." I can hear Brandon's smile through the phone, and I take on a little bit of a grin myself. This idea is his baby, and it's no small thing to ask someone else to help you change the shitty diapers and teach them first words.

It's an honor, but I don't know if I'm up to jumping into the startup world again. What if I fuck it up again? The stakes are even higher here. "Man, I'm really happy for you, but this is a lot to take in."

"I know, I know… This is an in-person sort of ask, but I couldn't sit on seven figures in the bank without calling you up immediately. Seriously, I should give you the login just so you can go stare at it for a while."

I laugh. It is pretty magical to stare at that many zeros in a bank account that's attached to your dream. It's validation you've got an idea worth pursuing. The problem is you have to keep momentum soaring up, because if gravity gets ahold of you, it's a long way down. Everything breaks when you free fall from that high up.

I don't have to say anything; Brandon's known me for long enough to understand my silence. "Okay, I know I threw down a lot. Just think about it. Don't say yes or no. I need to fly up to New York for the rest of the week to wrap up some contracts with my current job. I'll catch you when I get back to town."

"That sounds great," I say earnestly. I honestly don't know what I'll say at the end of the week, but I know I have to think this through. We hang up and I close my laptop, then I have the overwhelming urge to call Zoey and talk to her. I want to tell her about this job. I want to hear her opinion.

This is ridiculous. I'm not going to let my sister scare me into hiding. The damage is already done. I might as well go sift through the rubble and find the gems before someone else loots them.

I shove my laptop over onto the couch and make my way outside toward the double doors of the main house. I want to jump around and shake out my nerves, but I see Sam and Stewart just inside. I don't want Sam to know she's riled me before I even step inside. Besides, she won't rip out my intestines until after Stewart goes to bed. I have another three hours to make my getaway.

I brace myself as I open the door, but I'm met with silence. Even Stewart doesn't respond. *Strange.* "Um, hi?"

Stewart looks over, a big frown on his face. "Mommy said we're mad at you. I don't know why." Sam closes her eyes and takes a deep breath. I don't think she intended for him to repeat that, but she never has been a whiz at understanding that little kids don't operate under the same rules big kids do. There's no such thing as secret keeping with the under-five set.

I bend down to get eye level with him. "Ah, you're mad at me, huh? Well, maybe we can fix that. Why don't you go upstairs and work on our Lego fortress while your mom and I talk?"

Stewart nods his head and races upstairs. I stand up straight and look at Sam. Her eyes are fixed on me like a target, and I suddenly wonder if maybe I should have kept her kryptonite close by.

"I'm sorry I crossed the line with Zoey." I have no idea what Sam knows or what she think she knows, but I'm not going to wait for her to spill. I'm handing over as ambiguous a peace offering as I can.

Sam's face doesn't shift even a millimeter. "That's okay, I already called and fired her while Stewart was napping. I'm in the process of hiring a new nanny. I'll make sure this one isn't young and attractive."

Shit. She did fire Zoey. I thought Sam might do that, but I was hoping that somehow she was just taking the day off to think it through. I should have known better. "It's not her fault, Sam." I still can't stop myself from trying to reason with her.

"Yes, it is. She acted inappropriately. I don't care who started it. I will not tolerate that kind of behavior around my son."

Fuck, that's fair. I should have thought this through before I started trying to logic with a lawyer. I am so out of my league here. "Shouldn't you at least give her a second chance? I'll stay out of her way. I can move out if you want."

I don't have to wait for Sam's answer. "Not a chance." Her face is still glued in place.

"Don't you think you're being a little harsh? Zoey is a great nanny, and she clearly loves Stewart." I try to keep my breathing slow and calm, but I can feel my muscles tensing up like I'm about to enter the ring. I know why Sam is doing this, but it doesn't change the fact that it pisses me off. How am I related to such a hard-ass?

Sam just shakes her head. "Are we done with this conversation now?"

I can't stop my fingers from wrapping tightly inward. "You're so unforgiving. You're worse than Dad." It's a low blow, but I can't help it. She didn't even bother to ask what was going on. I want to tell her Zoey has two kids she's raising on her own, but I know it won't help. Sam isn't going to budge.

Sam slaps both of her hands down on the counter and I flinch in surprise. "I'm a mom, Elliott. I don't get to fuck around and move in with family because I can't get my shit together. I have to do what's best for Stewart, and if you cared at all about Zoey keeping her job, you should have stayed the hell away. It's not okay for someone that works for me to have a romantic relationship that could negatively impact my child. End of story. So, suck it up and deal with it, Elliott. Stop running around like a kid and then getting pissed off because you're living in the adult world."

It's strange to hear Sam swear. She's always in control, and even before Stewart, she was never the sailor-mouth type. But, it isn't the language she used that feels like a sharp blade—it's the truth she just sliced me open with.

I don't know what to say. I need to get out of here. "Are you and Stewart set for dinner?" It's become a habit for me to cook for them, but I don't even think I could put two pieces of bread and peanut butter together in my current state.

My sister nods and I take that as my cue. I walk out the French doors and pull out my phone. She's right. I need to grow up and be a goddamn adult for once.

Starting with getting my own set of wheels—hubcaps and exhaust pipes included.

Chapter 42

Zoey

It's already been twenty-four hours, and it still feels surreal that I got fired. I spent the day applying for jobs and making dinner. Who knew a homemade mac and cheese recipe would take practically three hours? Good thing I plan on being a working woman, because I definitely don't have the chops to be the main chef in my household. Maybe I should start tricking the girls into watching *Top Chef Junior* for inspiration.

We're halfway through finishing up dishes when I hear my phone. I wipe off my hands and pick it up just in time to see Elliott's name flash across the screen with a text before it goes black.

Are you free?

I quickly swipe it open and type yes before I even think it through. Fortunately, my mom and sister are here so I know the girls are covered. I have no idea what I'm going to say to Elliott, but I'm going to have to figure this out as I go.

"I need to pop outside for a second," I say to no one in particular.

My mom and Cassie nod and the girls continue to wipe down the table. It's a five-second job that takes them practically ten minutes. If I didn't know better, I'd think they were trying to scam us into only having to do one chore. It's just the way kid time works. Every task takes them a hundred times longer than it would take an adult. This is one of those times when their sluggish pace is working in my favor.

I step outside and see Elliott immediately, leaning against a bright red Honda Civic like some modern day Jake Ryan.

I don't have a bridesmaid dress on—in fact, my well-worn pajamas are pretty much the polar opposite—but I still feel like I'm walking right into a movie, and I like where it's headed.

I get a few steps closer and realize he's holding a bag of Oreos and a bottle of wine. Oh, this is getting better by the second.

When I'm a step away, he holds them out to me. "I heard you lost your job. I thought I would bring these by to cheer you up." I can tell he's trying to hold back a smile, but the corners of his mouth turn up in protest.

My nerves blend into my excitement—everything is aflutter and I wonder if I'll be able to keep two feet on the ground.

"It's okay, my boss was kind of intense, and I kind of fell for her brother."

Elliott can't hold back his smile any longer. "Just kind of?"

My heart wants me to say I'm falling for him, but my head is just trying to catch up to the I'm-fired-and-you're-standing-outside-my-house whirlwind. I settle somewhere in the middle and tilt my head to the side with a little raise of my shoulder and a playful smirk. "How'd you know I like Oreos and wine?"

"I was paying attention to your cart when I saw you at the grocery store. Did I do okay?" His question is innocent, but the way his eyes drop down at the edges makes me think he's nervous about this grand gesture.

"This is perfect."

"Well, I was going for cheesy eighties movie here with the red car and the just-say-yes moment. I couldn't snag a stereo and trench coat on short notice though."

"That would have really pulled the scene together," I say with a sarcastically straight face that only lasts for two seconds. Inside, my heart is doing cartwheels. He made a moment, just for me.

"Can I ask you something?" he starts and I nod, already knowing what I will say but feeling my nerves ratchet up anyway. "Will you say yes now?"

There's only one answer to this. I take a step in, wrap my arms around his neck, and press my lips firmly to his in an unspoken but shockingly clear yes.

It doesn't take him more than a beat to wrap his arms around my waist and press his body against mine in happy acceptance of my response.

He pulls away a moment later and looks at me like I'm a birthday gift wrapped up in a bow—all excitement and appreciation.

"I know it might not be an easy day for you, but it's easily one of my best."

"Eh, it's worth it," I tell him with a sideways smile.

Elliott hasn't let go of me and I'm content to stand here in his arms all day, but it's only going to be a few more minutes before Phoebe and Louisa start wondering where I went. I don't need to add explaining this to the list of discussion topics I already have for them.

"I need to get back inside."

Elliott doesn't argue. He kisses the top of my forehead and unwraps his arms from around my waist. He's not a parent, but I already get the sense that he gets that some of the rules are very different. "Can I take you out this Friday?"

"Like, at night?" I ask like a total newbie.

Elliott laughs and nods as he opens his car door.

"It's a date." It really is, and as I head back to the house, I practically skip the whole way.

Chapter 43

Zoey

It's a slow crawl until Friday. I spend as much time as I can with the girls, but they loved camp so much, they begged Cassie to take them back. I would love to exclusively sit and binge on *Gilmore Girls* while doing homework, but I use my extra time to start applying to jobs. I still haven't heard back about the competition and the internship promised to the winner. I know I have a solid entry, but I really can't put all my eggs in one basket.

So, I work on my online resume and portfolio and send it off to every company and position I'm remotely qualified for.

It takes up a lot of time, but it's mindless. It's the same questions over and over: name, education, qualifications, etc. I've typed, clicked, and selected my way across over two dozen applications.

The entire time, I'm thinking about Friday. It was so easy to say yes.

It's a lot harder to sit around after that yes and think about how completely unqualified I am for the dating scene. My dance card has been embarrassingly slim these past few years. A year ago, I went out to lunch with a guy I was friends with back in grade school, and I realized later that he thought it was a date while I just thought it was catching up. It was lunch for heaven's sake; it doesn't get any more friend-zoned than that.

Going out with Elliott on Friday is definitely not the friend zone.

What if I'm a deer in the headlights of a really good-looking, all features loaded car? This whole time, he's been the guy I couldn't possibly date. There was no pressure.

Now, I am dating him, and I have no idea how to act natural.

If we're talking about qualifications, I'm absolutely, not at all even in the applicant pool for what comes after. My sexual prowess is zilch. I lucked out with that incident in the pool. I didn't have time to think. I didn't even have time to count the number of dudes I'd had sex with.

Which is a whopping grand total of two.

I know. I feel like pretty much the only person on this side of the Kardashian era who can count their hookups on one hand. I've never had time to be embarrassed about it before. It's not like having two four-year-olds really leaves one with an excess of time to meet men.

And let's be real, my vagina was simply not open for business for at least a year and a half after the whole pushing-not-one-but-two-little-watermelons-out deal.

No, thank you.

I know nothing about having good sex outside what I've learned from the movies—which basically amounts to nothing useful besides an appreciation for good lighting and body doubles, and knowing fake orgasms really do sound fake. So basically, I'm screwed in actually getting screwed.

I wish I had thought about this before saying yes, but I know if I called—okay, yes, I'd probably be a chicken and text—to say I felt sick, he'd just reschedule. I can't rain check my way out of this.

On Friday night, I tell the girls I'm having dinner with a friend and drive to downtown Chapel Hill. Elliott offered to pick me up, but I don't want to risk accidentally involving Phoebe and Louisa. Not yet.

I'm wearing the only sundress I own, along with matching underwear—even though I'm tempted to Bridget Jones the situation with one of the many pairs of dreadfully overused granny panties I own. What? They are comfortable with a capital C.

I recognize that they didn't actually do Bridget any good, so here I am with sweet pink lace cheekies and a matching bralette. As I get out of the car, I keep tugging my dress down. Every hint of wind dares to showcase where this date might lead.

God, I'm such an amateur.

At least I snagged a clutch parking spot so the walk to the restaurant is short. When I make it through the door with no wardrobe malfunctions, I practically want to do a touchdown dance. Fortunately, I'm distracted by the delicious aroma of food. *Mmm.* Elliott did well picking this spot. I can't wait to stuff my face with Indian food—oh wait, I'm on a date. Okay, I can't wait to politely nibble on amazing Indian food. Better?

I see Elliott toward the back. He stands up and by the way he looks me, I swear he thinks I look more delicious than this place smells.

"Hi." He smiles and pulls out a chair for me, and I swoon. Yup, I'm glad I decided to be reasonable and go with flats tonight. I cannot trust my knees to be of very much help.

Speaking of which, I quickly scan the drinks menu. The first thing with gin that catches my eye is a winner. You can't go wrong with gin.

"How's the—" I start.

"So you—" he starts, our words overlapping.

I laugh nervously and reach for my water. "You first."

"It's lame small talk," he says, shaking his head. "I was going to ask if you found a parking spot okay, but you're five minutes early to my fifteen…you obviously found parking."

I smile and nod my head in nonchalant confirmation.

"I'm nervous." His smile is casual but his eyes are serious. "I haven't been nervous on a date in a very long time. I don't think I would have even admitted that before, but this isn't your average first date."

"We didn't exactly meet at a bar. You didn't give me some ridiculous yet endearing pickup line. I didn't give you my phone number and want you to text after three hours instead of three days."

"And we didn't meet on a dating site where both of our profiles were a bit more flattering than real life."

That idea sends shivers down my spine, and not the good kind. I've been one tight breath away from an anxiety attack all day, and Elliott is a far cry from a perfect stranger. The perspective is good. I know Elliott. He makes me nervous, but it's more what's-gonna-happen than is-he-secretly-married-with-five-kids.

I reach out my hand and interlace my fingers through his. "Don't be nervous. You've already seen me naked." I don't know where that brazen humor came from, but I'll take it.

Elliott chuckles and squeezes my hand back, and I know in an instant that tonight is going to be a magical sparkly unicorn in a world of donkey-ass first dates.

Chapter 44

Elliott

As I stare at the woman sitting across from me, I am entranced by her. I don't know how I got to be the lucky one sitting in this chair, but I'm damn glad I won this lottery.

She's witty and open and sexy as hell. The little sundress she's wearing is driving me crazy with its trail of buttons running from stunning top to tempting bottom. I want to take my time unthreading every single one of them, and yet I know I'm just as likely to rip them apart like curtains standing between me and unrestricted access to pure sunlight.

Our waiter comes over to remove our dinner plates. "May I interest you two in dessert this evening?"

I can tell by the twinkle in Zoey's eyes that the answer to that question is a yes. I give her a nod with a smile to let her know I'm interested in dessert too.

And everything that comes after.

She orders the chai cheesecake without even having to look at the menu again. I order the cardamom rice pudding and turn back to face the woman who has kept my attention all night without even trying.

"Okay, first kiss."

Zoey crinkles her nose playfully. "Ninth grade, behind the tennis courts before school. His name was Daniel, and he used so much tongue it was like getting licked by a puppy. We went out for two whole weeks, and it never got any better." She leans forward as if we're coconspirators. "And you?"

I take a sip of my drink and smile with a hint of pride. "Eighth grade. Ashley Kantis. Everyone was getting on their bus on the last day of school. I ran after her and asked her to go steady with me over the summer, and when she said yes, I kissed her. Everyone saw. I was the hero of my bus route that day."

Zoey shares my smile. "And what happened to Ashley?"

"She dumped me a week later for the neighborhood pool lifeguard that had just finished ninth grade. I think they got married and had a bunch of kids."

"How very *Sandlot* of them."

I knew I liked this girl. "That movie is one of my all-time favorites."

"You're male. I think it's practically required that you love that movie."

"True. What's yours?"

"*Beauty and the Beast.* I pretty much want to live in the scene where they bring her all the food and sing to her while she taste tests it all. I would be in heaven."

As if on cue, the waiter brings out our desserts. Zoey's eyes grow wide with delight, and I make a note to never buy her flowers. Clearly, appealing to her stomach is the winning route.

Zoey takes a bite of her cheesecake and closes her eyes with a soft murmur. She breaks off another piece, presses it to her lips, and then stops abruptly. "Aren't you going to eat yours?"

I haven't even lifted my spoon yet. "I think it might be even better if I just watch you enjoy yours."

Zoey blushes. "It's really good. You want a bite?"

"Sure." I know it won't be as good as leaning over and taking a taste of those sweet lips, but I don't think there's anything that can compete with that.

Zoey presses her fork through the soft crust again and holds it out for me. Somehow, it feels like our fiftieth date and our first date at the same time.

I take the bite without taking my eyes off Zoey.

I'm falling in love with her, and instead of scaring me, it feels exhilarating, as if I'm finally taking the first step into the rest of my life.

Chapter 45

Zoey

After dinner, I walk out with Elliott to his car, which is parked a bit before mine, and we linger at the passenger door. Neither one of us wants the night to end. Two drinks over the course of two hours isn't enough to get me drunk, but it's enough to remove any filter.

"I wish I didn't have to go."

Elliott leans in toward me, tracing my jaw with his finger. His eyes are locked on my lips. "Do you have to?"

I think it through. Both my mom and sister are home. Logistically, the answer is no, but where are we going to go? There's no way I'm taking Elliott home with me, and I'm not going to get caught sneaking through the backyard of my former employer.

As if on cue, Elliott's lips turn up in a devious smirk. "What if I told you there was a secret entrance to the pool house?"

My pulse picks up. "I'd say I'd be interested…"

"I couldn't agree more." He grabs the door handle and pulls the door open for me. "Come back to my place, then."

I nod, my throat suddenly feeling as dry as a desert. I try swallowing, but it barely helps. My body is going haywire with electric pulses of excitement and nerves.

Once we're both in the car, I try to focus on the route as if I were driving. Red lights are hell, because when there's a pause in activity, my brain starts to cycle through the revolving door of thoughts.

I haven't had sex in years—oh god. I'm probably worse than a virgin—he'll assume I have some inkling of experience so the expectations are higher, but my ability is probably more akin to someone who hasn't even jumped in the sack. Are we even going to have sex? What's the proper amount of making out time? Tongue? No tongue? Ah!

It's one long word-vomit of negative self-talk. I wish I had a little imaginary *Sex in the City* cast in my life to send me into the sex arena with a loving smack on the tush and a quick pep talk to tell me to go get 'em.

It doesn't help that Elliott is absolutely silent. By the fifth red light, I can't take it any more.

"What are you thinking about?" I probe nervously. On the first light, I didn't want to know, but when I couldn't get my own brain to pipe down on lights two through four, I gave up. I'd rather hear that he regrets getting in the car than deal with my own thoughts for another thirty seconds.

"How to keep myself from pulling over so I can kiss you already."

My mouth forms a perfectly round *oh.*

That effectively shuts down the freak-out train while my imagination takes over, and I visualize myself crawling over the console to straddle him and letting him pull my dress over my head.

A car honks behind us. I swallow audibly and point ahead. "It's green."

Elliott presses the gas a little harder than intended, intent on getting us to point B a heck of a lot faster now, and the car lurches forward. He awkwardly mumbles an apology, and I can't help but smile.

Minutes later, we pull through the gated entrance with a few presses of the buttons on the keypad, but Elliott takes a left instead of the usual right. He winds through a few unfamiliar turns, and finally we stop in front of a house that is most definitely not the one his pool house belongs to.

I eye the mansion looming behind a neatly trimmed lawn. "We're not breaking and entering while somebody's on vacation, right?"

"Would you, if I asked?" He smiles wickedly.

In my current worked-up state? "Probably." But, I want to be prepared for all potential felonies. "Are we?"

"No, just a little trespassing, not full on B&E tonight."

He gets out of the car and I follow, plodding across the bright green grass. We head toward the shrubs that line the perimeter of this yard. I wonder for a brief moment if it's a good idea, but I force that thought into a deep dark corner of my mind. If I start asking if one thing's a good idea, it might start a whole domino chain that rivals an OK Go music video.

No. Instead, I reach for Elliott's hand. When I catch it, he stops and turns around to give me a look that's a mix of adolescent mischief and joy.

All I have to do is stop and focus on him, blinders on to block out the rest of the world, and I remember exactly why I'm tiptoeing through a random stranger's lawn at dusk.

The reason is the most captivating man I've ever met. Elliott MacCallister is good for my soul.

Suddenly, there's a small break in the dense shrubs where the side perimeter meets the back. There's a large flat stone that's set into the ground, like a path between the end of one yard to another.

"Did you do that?" I wonder aloud. It makes no sense, but it's just plain strange to connect the backyards of two random houses.

Elliott chuckles softly. "No. When these houses were first built, the two owners each had kids the same age so they had a pathway put in. My sister bought the house when one family moved up to DC, but the original owners still live here." He pauses to point back at the house we just passed. "I met them on a run and they told me about it."

"So, they know you use it?"

"Eh, not exactly, but I'm pretty sure they wouldn't press charges." I can tell he's teasing by the way his eyes crinkle at the sides with devilish delight. I step through the opening quickly all the same.

"Come on, this way." Elliott squeezes my hand and leads me toward the shadowed outline of the pool house.

We walk up to the wood paneling of the outdoor shower. I never used it in all the times Stewart and I played out here. I always defaulted to the priority of getting the little man back inside and into dry clothes.

Elliott unlatches one of the panels, swinging it open to reveal a tiled shower that sits right next to the sliding glass doors of a matching indoor shower. Elliott pushes that door open. "Voila!" he says with mock showmanship. "It's not a grand entrance, but it's definitely a secret one."

As I step out of the bathroom into the main living area of the pool house, all I can wonder is if there's a foolproof way to conjure up an out-of-body experience.

Because I would pay buckets of money for some autopilot right now—and not the been married for ten years with three kids, same position, two minutes and you're done sort of autopilot.

I'm talking the effortlessly floating above while everything is drenched in a shimmering marigold light, and it's so wistfully perfect you're reasonably sure you've just reached nirvana kind.

Yeah, how do I switch on that kind of autopilot?

"Come here," Elliott says smoothly. Even though I'm standing halfway across the room, his pheromones are practically knocking me out from here.

My mind quickly runs through its fight or flight options. *Run and you're turning down what is potentially the greatest sex of your life. Stay and you risk exposing yourself as an awkward jellyfish—and let me tell you, no one wants to have sex with a jellyfish.* I don't know if I'll survive the embarrassment.

I nervously twirl one of the buttons on the front of my dress. I can feel my lungs jump as I try to pull air in and out.

Elliott takes a step back toward me and reaches out his hand. I want to run, but I also don't want to walk away from him. The dichotomy is maddening. He's everything I want and everything I'm scared of.

I quickly take an internal vote. Lady parts vote stay. Head votes go. Legs remain decidedly neutral. I let go of the button and weave my fingers through his. His grip is soft but firm, and he uses it to pull the rest of me in close.

I pull in a surprised breath and get a strong dose of Elliott musk. It's like everything good in a kitchen mixed with a camping trip. *Damn, that's good.*

"I'm glad you came home with me." Elliott tucks a strand of hair behind my ear and his fingers linger at my earlobe, tracing its outline. His eyes never leave mine, and they're heavy with need. For me.

Why does that feel so good? Well, maybe because a guy that could easily qualify for a *People's Sexiest* cover has me in his arms and wants to keep me there. I want to give myself a fist bump.

I'd say every woman should have an Elliott, but I'm really not into a group share option here.

Elliott lowers his hand to explore the curve where my shoulder meets my neck. "I can see the thoughts running through your head, but I have no idea what you're thinking."

Um, how I'm so not the sex goddess you were probably hoping for. "I'm just nervous." Honest, but less embarrassing than admitting the full truth.

"Don't worry, there's no one here to score our performance."

I shudder with a small laugh. Yeah, thank god this isn't a spectator sport. "It's been a long time," I finally admit.

Elliott squeezes my shoulder gently. "It's okay. We'll go slow."

Oh god, awkward jellyfish in slow motion? That might be worse.

"You look like I just suggested having sex on a bed of rotten eggs."

I don't know, that might be better. I feel the admission sitting on my throat. It's getting heavier by the second. I know I just need to toss it out there. I stare into the espresso swirls of Elliott's eyes, and it's just the shot of caffeine I need. "I might be awful—scratch that, I know I'm going to be awful."

Elliott laughs. "I'm not looking for porn star-worthy sex here, Zoey. I'm a guy. We're not all that picky, and hell, I'm up for all the practice you can handle."

The weight I've been carrying around for the past few days starts to melt away, like a rock disintegrating into sand. I let it fall off of me. "Are you sure?"

"Yes." His answer is so sure, so solid, I have to believe him.

I want to kiss his honesty right there on the spot. It's disarming and comforting and absolutely everything I need in this moment. I open up the door to my thoughts and let him in.

"I don't want to screw this up."

I can see Elliott swallow slowly. "That's not possible. You drew me into your gravitational pull, and now I never want to leave."

"I fought that feeling," I admit quietly. "I don't want to any more."

"Good." He leans in, his lips a breath away from mine. "Because you're my sun now."

The distance is closed in an instant, like a seal to a promise. He is mine.

And I am his.

I press the full length of my body to his and nip his lip with the tip of my teeth.

I step away from him and begin to open each of the tiny buttons that trail down the front of my dress. When I get to the button just above my belly button, I stop to let the dress fall to a pool around my feet. I feel every single cell in blissful motion, and yet it's like I've become a spectator in my own body. I don't know where this confidence is coming from, but I'll take it.

I can see Elliott's breath become a shallow staccato. I've never done this to a man before, but if this is what it feels like to turn someone on, I'd do it every damn day. There's something so intoxicating about watching desire flood his entire body, filling every corner with need for me.

Elliott sits down on the couch and I drift over to him, lowering myself down to rest my legs in a straddle on each side of his. His arms wrap around my waist and I lean down to wrap my own around the base of his neck.

I want him. All of him.

I reach down and grab the hem of his shirt to lift it off, breaking our contact for only a second. He moves his hands to the hooks of my bra and unlatches it, tracing the outline of my shoulders and arms while he slips it off.

I pull back, unable to resist the urge to gaze over the perfection that's right in front of me. Elliott's muscular chest leads down to abs that would make Michael Phelps cry. Even sitting, I can see the two angled lines that point like a neon flashing arrow.

Oh yes, I'm going there. Don't you worry, dear arrow.

I glance back up and lock eyes with Elliott while I work my way to his belt, and he smiles with mild amusement. I am one hundred percent objectifying him, and he has no issue with that.

His hands begin to move up my thighs, drawing his fingers along the curving lines of my hips and waist until his thumbs meet the sweet nip of skin along my breasts. He begins to trace in until he reaches the buds in the center. My already shallow breath stops altogether.

Elliott reaches down to meet one of his thumbs with his tongue. *Oh god, this feels so damn good.* I want more. I want to release the pressure building inside me. I get back to undoing his belt and peeling the button and zipper open. I can feel the length of him hard against my hand.

I trace its outline as I whisper into his ear, "I want you inside me." I feel a tiny shudder run through his body at my words.

Elliott's hand lifts up to meet mine and in one fluid motion he wraps my legs around his waist, stands up, and carries me over to the bedroom.

Lowering me down onto the bed, he slips his pants off and then meets me on top of the soft sheets. Instead of pressing his body to match the length of mine, he starts to trail kisses from my ankle up the sensitive inner line of my leg, like tiny shocks of pleasure. Their intensity builds until he reaches the light pink lace hem at the top of my thigh. He traces it with his fingers and when he reaches the top, he peels it down to reveal the last bit of covered flesh.

His mouth reaches the spot where it all meets together in a cluster of live wires. He flicks his tongue against me in a soft, sweeping crescendo and the dam breaks open, releasing the flood of pressure through my body in an overwhelming wave.

I look up and see Elliott gazing up at me with a wicked smile playing across his lips. I never want to leave this bed again, and he knows it.

He crawls up and presses his body against mine. All at once, it's too much and not enough. I pull him in tightly and kiss him like I need him more than air.

I open my eyes and see the same desire heavy in his eyes.

Elliott positions himself against me. "Are you ready?"

"Yes."

In that moment, time stands still. The only thing that moves is the release of my long dormant muscles as they envelop him so completely I swear we're no longer two separate bodies.

We move together as I feel the wave of pressure begin to pitch again. This time Elliott's ragged breath matches mine.

I arch my back and everything fades away but the feeling that my body is breaking apart and being put back together piece by exquisite piece.

When I meet reality again, Elliott is next to me with an untamed grin on his face. I know the feeling, and it's a damn good one. I snuggle into the warmth of his side, wrapping my leg around his.

Elliott reaches over and runs his fingers up and down my arm in a calming rhythm. "See, it's just like riding a bike."

I barely hold back a laugh. "Damn, I'd ride bikes more often if it felt that good."

"I think another round can be arranged."

"I'll take as many rounds as you can handle." I'd give up all the food in the world to have an infinite supply of this—exactly this moment—and when I look into his eyes, I know he feels the same way.

Elliott flips onto his stomach and pulls me tight against him. Yup, he's definitely on for round two. "I'm in."

"Okay, cowboy, you're on." I press my lips to his with a bold smile. I like what we started this evening, and I think I'm going to love where we're headed even more.

Chapter 46

Zoey

My eyes flutter open and it takes me a moment to thread together the pieces of my surroundings. I am covered in an unfamiliar soft sheet and definitely one hundred percent naked. There's a soft stream of light crossing the head of the bed and my limbs are wrapped around a hard, warm body.

My mind finally wakes up and the memory of last night streams in vivid Technicolor.

Shit buckets. Last night—as in, it's currently morning.

I jerk upright and try to remember where I put my phone. I see the tiny hands of the vintage alarm clock on the bedside table. 6:45am.

Oh, this is not good. I can't believe I fell asleep.

Granted, I'm sure this is the direct result of the first non-self-induced orgasm in years…and the dozen that came after. That shit really is better than Nyquil.

I jump out of bed and race out to the living room to grab my purse. I find it by the door of the bathroom and dig in to find my phone.

No messages.

Good. Okay, I still have a shot at getting home before anyone notices, but I need to move—fast. I peel my dress and bra off the floor and start to pull myself together. I make my way back to the bedroom to grab my underwear and Elliott meets me at the doorway. He leans down and kisses me sweetly.

He would totally make me we-finally-had-sex pancakes. I wish I had time, but I am two seconds away from a where's-mommy situation.

"Morning." He softens my nerves that are starting to frazzle from my unintended sleepover.

"I need to get home," I say apologetically. I wish I could stay, but that's not how my life works.

"I can drive you back to your car," Elliott offers, turning back to the bedroom to get his clothes.

I think it through. By the time I get into downtown, grab my car, and then drive home, it might be 8am. "Actually, can you take me to my house? I'll have my sister drive me to my car later today."

"No problem."

We're through our secret entrance and inside Elliott's car within two minutes. I keep my phone on my lap, anxiously awaiting a ding that will tell me my absence at home has been noticed.

As we pull up to the house, my phone is still silent. Even so, I jump out of the car, eager to get inside so I can change into my pajamas and pretend like I just woke up in my own bed.

229

Elliott meets me around the side of the car and pulls me in for a kiss. I sink into the pleasant feeling of satisfaction before I remember I'm less than a hundred yards away from two little people that have no idea their mom is in the middle of falling in love.

"I wish I could stay…" I unwrap my arms from around Elliott even though I desperately want to stay there and soak in more of this morning-after nirvana.

"It's okay." He reaches out and runs his thumb gently along the line of my jaw. "We're going to have a million more mornings to spend together."

The thought leaves me speechless. I hadn't stopped to think about the future yet, but the idea of more mornings—slower ones that we can savor—is like a Mayfair-filtered image in my mind. It may not be reality, but it sure does look amazing from this side of the screen.

"Go," Elliott urges, his eyes bright. "Go pretend you got home last night."

I give him a quick smile and dash toward the side door. I hear his car start to hum as he slowly pulls away, and I gently shut the door behind me.

A flash of color catches my eye, and I see Phoebe coming toward me in a quick run.

"Morning, Mama!" she cries out. Louisa is leaning against the back of the couch looking out the window. "We woke up early and you weren't home."

My throat is dry, but I manage to swallow enough to ask, "Are

Grandma and Aunt Cassie awake yet?"

"Nope!"

I walk over to Louisa and sit down. One of the biggest differences between the two of them is that Phoebe is a doer and Louisa is a thinker. She's processing, and I just have to sit patiently and wait for her to piece through her thoughts. My nerves are anything but patient, and I have to clamp my teeth down on the inner corner of my cheek to stay silent.

Louisa finally looks over at me. "Did you have a sleepover last night?"

"Sort of," I answer as honestly as I can. "I didn't mean to, but I was so tired I accidentally fell asleep."

She nods. "Was that our dad?"

Her question slams me against a brick wall I didn't even know I was standing in front of.

I'm not ready to answer this question or the web of questions that spiral infinitely out from the heart of this curiosity like razor-thin threads.

"No, that wasn't your dad." I wonder for a moment if she recognized Elliott from their brief meeting at the grocery store.

"Are we going to meet our dad?"

The wounds from my own fatherless childhood stir awake after years of undisturbed quiet. I know exactly how her questions feel; they're like a heavy stone. Mine has rounded over the years, but hers is still so raw and full of jagged edges. I can help round the corners, but it's a long process that will take years.

"I don't know, honey." I don't know if Nathan will ever be

231

enough of a man to be a regular part of their life. I'm not going to let him flit in and out like an unreliable jerk.

"Who was that this morning, then?" Louisa shifts, and it strikes me right next to where the original question hit.

"A friend of mine," I answer softly, barely able to get those few words out. I feel like I'm sinking into mental quicksand. I won't let Nathan around until he can prove he's a good role model and able to be a consistent part of their lives, so how can I hold Elliott to any less of a standard?

What kind of relationship can stand up to that level of pressure? Certainly not one that's just finding its sea legs. It's like sending a tiny little sailboat into the middle of the ocean in a violent hurricane; there would be no hope of surviving.

"Are we going to meet him?" Louisa echoes my train of thought in an odd sort of déjà vu.

"I don't think so." I reach out and give her a kiss on the forehead where her brows are crinkled together with thoughts much too heavy for a four-year-old. "Let's have pancakes this morning," I offer in a thinly veiled bribe: their favorite breakfast for an undisputed change in topic.

I'll get my pancakes, just not cooked to order by the dreamboat who drove me home this morning. Sometimes, being an adult really sucks.

Phoebe bounces over. She had been dancing around the outskirts of our conversation, but I know she picked up most of it from the crazy twin telepathy they share.

"Pancakes!" she shouts as she twirls around happily. I can feel

Louisa shift beside me, and I'm overwhelmingly grateful for the pull of Phoebe's joy.

"Want to help me make the batter?" Thank goodness making batter is about as easy as mixing water with that stuff that comes in a box. Even a moron in the kitchen and two pre-kindergarteners can't screw it up.

Louisa stays still for a moment, and then she nods and lets Phoebe tug her off the couch toward the kitchen. I watch them dance away together, and I wonder if this is what motherhood is...one sacrifice after another in order to protect our children? I almost can't stand from the weight, but I don't know what else to do. I can handle tending to my own wounds, but what if my daughters get hurt too? It would be too much.

"Can we make Mickey Mouse cakes, Mom?" Phoebe calls out.

They're already entranced by the task of making breakfast. I pinch myself and follow their lead, one foot in front of the other. Better to hurt a little now rather than a lot later.

Chapter 47

Elliott

I'm still buzzing with excitement when I meet Brandon for coffee on Saturday morning. In retrospect, it was probably a bad idea to order a large double-shot cappuccino. My legs are shaking like my own personal earthquake, but Brandon keeps walking me through the business plan he's drawn up like I'm not a sitting San Andreas over here.

"...which is why I need you as CEO while I sit as the Chief Operating Officer. I need to focus on the details of day-to-day operations while you act as the external figurehead of the company. I trust your business instinct and I know our investors would prefer to have someone with your background sitting at the head of the table."

I almost laugh out loud. "They know my last company failed, right?" I thought having the title of CEO on your resume was only a gold star when, I don't know, your company didn't crash and burn to the ground.

"I think you're underestimating the value of failure. Yeah, it sucks you had to shut down your company, but you also have a better idea of what to watch out for. You're not going to make the same mistakes twice, which makes you more capable of paving the way to success than CEOs who have never failed to begin with."

I don't know why I hadn't thought about it that way. I had been staring at the experience like it was a black mark on my career, but that's a one-dimensional explanation.

"So, what do you think?"

What do I think? I think I'm on top of the fucking world. I got the girl. I finally feel like I can take on the job, and hey, I even got the used car guy to bump it down by 2K. "I'm in."

Brandon nods his head and gives me a smile as big as Texas. "Good, because I was going to blackmail you if you said no."

You know, I wouldn't put it past him. Once he has an idea, he uses everything he's got to make it a reality. I know he's going to bring this idea of his to life, and I not only respect the hell out of him for it, I want to be there supporting his vision every step of the way. "Okay, get the lawyer I know you have on speed dial to draw up a contract and we'll hash out the details—although from everything you've said, I think we're on the same page."

Brandon reaches into his tan leather messenger bag and pulls out a quarter-inch thick stack of papers. "Good, because I already had her draw it up."

I should have known. I take the contract from him and thumb through it with a smile.

"Take a few days, read it over, have your sister look over it, and then let me know what you think."

"I don't think Sam is going to be doing me any favors any time soon."

Brandon cocks his head to the side inquisitively. We've been all business this morning. I haven't mentioned anything about the past few days. I proceed to give him the rough outline and when I finish, he responds with a low whistle. "So, do I need to thank Zoey for you saying yes today?"

A smile sneaks up on me. I knew I was going to say yes before I walked in today; I wouldn't have wasted Brandon's time if I didn't think it was a serious option. I didn't really mentally dive deep into my motivation, but now that he mentions it, Zoey certainly is a large piece. It's time for me to get back up on my feet, and even though I'm using my own two legs to do it, it's possible because she's standing in the foreground of my big picture.

Chapter 48

Zoey

I look down at my phone for the twenty millionth time, again rereading the string of messages Elliott has sent me over the past few days.

Saturday, July 26

I had a really great time last night.

Sunday, July 27

Are you free at all this week?

Monday, July 28

Is everything okay?

Tuesday, July 29

Are you alive?

I don't want to be a stalker and just show up at your house.

I'm worried about you.

Sorry. Yes, I'm alive.

Whew. Okay.

Had me worried.

Are you free tonight?

Or tomorrow?

Hell, any time? :)

Wednesday, July 30

Okay, now I'm really thinking about stopping by.

What's going on, Z?

Talk to me.

Please don't.

I need time.

Friday, August 1

Can we talk?

This radio silence is driving me crazy.

I wish I could talk. My brain hasn't stopped running all over the place, and it's definitely not running laps—more like ridiculous overlapping squiggles that make no sense. I don't know if I have the capacity to translate my thoughts into coherent conversation material.

And honestly, I'm not ready to hear the words yet. It'll be real once they escape into the air between us. I won't be able take them back. So, here I am being a complete coward and avoiding reality for as long as radio silence will carry me.

My laptop purrs quietly on my lap like an overheating cat. It may have been saved from the cliff of death, but I swear it still peeks its head over from time to time. It dings at me, probably an auto-response email confirming my application to another job. I'm almost at the end of my list of graphic design companies that are hiring. I'll be onto the barista jobs of the world next.

I frown at the thought. I knew finding another job would be hard, but this silent slog through applications with nothing but template emails in return is soul-crushing.

We've received your application. We will review it and contact you if we think it's a good fit.

I want to punch every single auto-response bot in the digital face. Just tell me I'm the fifty millionth person to send you their information, that I'm not remotely qualified because I haven't even finished my degree yet, and that you're never going to get back to me.

Ever.

I am the queen of pity-party-ville. It's a real blast.

I click over to my email begrudgingly and see a response from Draper and Young, an advertising agency I applied to.

Zoey -

We are very impressed with your resume and portfolio. We would like to have you come by our office next week for an interview. Please send us a list of available times.

We look forward to hearing from you.

Warmly,

Chelsea Weston

Recruiting Coordinator

Draper and Young

My mood flutters up for a moment. An interview! Yes! Then my phone strums and it comes crashing back down when I see Elliott's name on my screen.

I'm coming to pick you up in an hour.

It strums again.

Meet me at the end of your block.

My cheeks turn red with outrage. He can't demand to see me. I have kids. I have a life. I can't drop everything to see him. I unlock my phone and start typing a reply when another bubble appears.

Please

It's enough to soften me, just a little. Okay, fine, so I'm currently still in my pajamas at two o'clock in the afternoon and the twins are off at drama camp again with Cassie.

I'm pissed because I don't want to do this, and I don't want to be forced. Elliott's calling my bluff now. I have the time, and if I put it off, he's going to keep bugging me. I type in four letters like I'm pounding away at a typewriter—deliberately and with way more force than a touchscreen needs.

Fine

That's the nicest four letters he's going to get from me.

I quickly send off a list of times to Draper and Young. I would have responded with an all caps ANY TIME YOU'LL HAVE ME, but I'm pretty sure interviews are like dating: overeager is the kiss of death. I need to play it cool. I respond with a few blocks of time and cross my fingers they didn't send the email to the wrong Zoey Porter.

I close down my computer, on to the next problem. I have no idea what you wear to break up with someone, but I'm pretty sure pajamas are not the look I'm going for.

That annoying little voice in my head tells me to just get this over with, but I tell it to go stuff its face in a freezer and hop in the shower to wash off five days worth of depression. Seriously, that isn't a good look for any amount of public consumption.

I'm getting this over with, and then I'm going to snap out of this funk and get back to real life.

I'm at the corner ten minutes early in case Elliott thinks I'm going to flake and drives all the way to my house.

I wish I had brought a book. We've used up our shared data for the month, so my phone is reduced to a device that can communicate with people and take pictures.

I don't really think I want to make breakup selfies a thing, so I sit on the curb and watch the single sprinkler in the lawn across the street go back and forth in a vain attempt to bring the yellowed grass back to life.

I want to yell *Just give it up already*, but I doubt the sprinkler would care and am pretty sure the owners would just think I'm crotchety or crazy. Or both.

At this point, I'm not really sure if they'd be wrong.

Elliott's car pulls up and he rolls down the window. "Want to grab coffee?"

I don't think there's anything I want less—a beverage that will only make me more jittery than I already am, surrounded by a bunch of people that can overhear our conversation. No, thank you.

He notices my hesitation. I'm sure the look on my face is a dead giveaway. He shifts the car into park, gets out, and walks around. "I saw a park down the road. We could walk?"

I nod in agreement and we make our way there. Both of us walk along, absorbed in our own thoughts. I can barely take a full breath. It feels like someone has clamped a thirty-pound weight around my ribcage.

When we get to the park, Elliott heads straight for a bench that faces the empty swing set. We've barely sat down when he speaks up. "You're avoiding me, and I can't figure out why. We had an amazing night, and then silence. What's going on?"

"It's too much," I finally say. It's not an explanation so much as the overwhelming feeling I'm dealing with.

"What's too much? Us? Your job? Getting a babysitter? What?" Elliott asks as he turns to face me. I can't look at him, but I can feel the heat of his stare. "Tell me what it is so I can fix it."

I can't sit still under his gaze, so I stand up, walk over to the swings just in front of us, and fiddle with the metal chain. "I don't think you can fix it."

He follows me and sits in the swing next to mine. "That's pretty pessimistic."

"No, I think it's realistic."

"What can't be fixed then? What's so beyond repair that you're willing to throw this away?"

"I have two daughters, and that makes this all really complicated."

"I know that." Elliott sighs like he already knew what I would say and was just waiting for me to put it out there. "You can't keep punishing yourself because you accidentally got pregnant."

"This isn't about punishing myself," I snap back. "This is about protecting them. They're starting to ask about their dad— who is a royal prick, by the way. It's hard enough to protect them from the damage of him not being in their lives or worse, showing up again only to leave when it doesn't suit him any more. I can't add another man who might not stick around into the mix." I still can't look at Elliott, but I know he doesn't like what I'm saying. I can feel his frustration building.

I know I'm destroying this, us—or at least what could have been us.

He leans forward on the swing and rests his elbows on his knees while he stares at me for an uncomfortable minute. Then he practically jumps up and pushes the swing away forcefully, the metal clanking in protest. It startles me and I look over to find his lips in the straightest line I've ever seen. He's breathing tightly through his nose in an unhelpful effort to stay calm.

"I don't know which pisses me off more—that you think I don't realize I'm not just dating you but your daughters too or that you think we're just some summer fling that is going to fizzle out! I never intended to sleep with you and walk away. I'm not that kind of guy."

"I know that," I answer quietly.

"Then trust me."

"I can't." It's that simple. I have never known a man in my life to stay. Not Nathan. Not Stewart's dad. Not my own father. Asking me to trust him is like asking me to lead him to Santa's workshop. I wouldn't have the first clue how to get there, and I'm not even sure if it exists at all.

Elliott sticks his face into his hands, like he's trying to block out the world in order to focus on coming up with a solution.

I wish I had one. I've struggled this whole week trying, and I'm standing here empty-handed. "I can't trust you because I'm just not programmed that way. What relationship can survive that? Every time we fight, every time you feel overwhelmed at the prospect of being dad material, every time you get frustrated that we can't spend more time together...it's a lot of pressure."

Elliott lowers his hands and he looks stunned. "You're not even giving me a chance to prove myself."

"No, I'm not, but can you honestly tell me you've thought— really thought—about being a stepdad?"

He looks at me like I've thrown a dagger straight at him. "That's not fair. You're just throwing all of this at me now."

"Nothing about this is fair, but that doesn't make it any less true. Are you ready to be a dad? Are you ready to sacrifice your needs for children? They aren't even your own."

"No," he answers in defeat. I should feel satisfied. This is what I've been waiting for, and yet it tastes like I just accidentally bit into a lemon thinking it was an orange.

"Exactly."

"So, this is over then?" His tone is flat. I want to scream at him. *Do something! Be pissed off. Fight for me.* But I can't make him fight for this, for us. If he's willing to walk away, I won't make him stay.

"I think so." I try to mirror his resignation.

"I guess that's it then." His eyes are pinched together in silent distress. I wonder if it feels like his heart is a glass paperweight being thrown off a skyscraper too. We're only moments from its shattering impact.

"I guess it is." I turn on my heels without another word. It's over, I tell myself. Neither of us were going to fight for it. Better it's done now, then.

It's not a very convincing statement, but with every step I take, my stubbornness seals my decision. I'm not going to fight for something that was destined to take us down anyway.

My heart finally hits the earth, fracturing into thousands of jagged little pieces.

Chapter 49

Zoey

The next week is painfully slow. Even with Phoebe and Louisa around during the day again after the end of their drama camp, time is trying to enact some form of water-droplet torture on me.

Breaking up with Elliott was the right thing to do, and although my conscious mind got the memo, my subconscious is still playing the Elliott loop every time it takes over. I've also been preparing for my interview, so my emotionally crippled state is punctuated by moments of extreme anxiety.

Basically, I'm a joy to be around.

I can check my interview off the list today. I just pulled into the parking lot and I'm five minutes early; at least I have that going for me.

I walk into the starkly modern entryway of Draper and Young and immediately feel out of place. The few people who are walking around look like they've stepped straight out of a perfectly filtered Instagram photo. Their outfits are trendy and borderline casual. One girl wears high-waisted bell-bottom jeans with a geometric print blouse and long sweater vest. Another girl is wearing a pencil skirt with a vintage arcade t-shirt. It's those types of outfits that make you nod your head, thinking, *Hey, I could wear that,* but when you go home and actually try to put similar items from your closet together, you look like the before pictures on one of those closet makeover shows.

I nervously tug at my own skirt, borrowed from my sister's still unpacked mess of a suitcase. I don't ever remember her wearing this skirt and matching jacket, but it was the only thing that could reasonably qualify as business attire in our house. I wonder now if this was an outfit she picked up for an audition as a Cinderella office assistant. This is definitely from the wrong side of the transformation.

I couldn't justify running out to buy a brand new outfit for an interview, but when I look down at my very 2005 pinstripe combo, I regret not stopping by a secondhand store this week.

This is an advertising agency, I scold myself. *You should be showing them you can at least advertise yourself.*

Strike one.

I tell the person at the front desk I'm here for an interview and they direct me to the waiting area, saying someone will be down for me soon.

A guy named Kristof retrieves me from the bank of chairs and I wonder for a minute if he's the person who's going to interview me or their assistant. I swear he looks younger than me. He has a total hipster vibe: thick glasses, Justin Timberlake haircut, and haphazardly cuffed jeans he probably spent ten minutes getting just right.

I bet if he flipped through the lineup of the radio stations in my car, he'd stop this interview on the spot.

Stop it! my inner mom shouts at me. He's not hiring you based on your pop culture preferences. This is a job interview, not a friendship application.

I try to tell myself to keep it together when we walk into his office—yup, his office. *Kristof Simon, Senior Artistic Director.*

I take stock of the obscure art lining the walls as he tells me to take a seat. He sits in the vintage leather chair next to a small round table rather than the one behind his desk. Who does that? This isn't a sit on the same side of the booth date. Why is this already so awkward?

He leans back on the two rear legs and clasps his hands together. "So, Zoey, I don't want to start out with the classic tell-me-about-yourself line. Let's talk about what inspires you instead. What are you into these days?"

Awesome. Replace one completely vague question for another. I take a deep breath. I should have taken him to my car and shown him my music collection. It would have been quicker.

Twenty minutes go by in a painfully slow crawl. I try to fall back on talking about what I've learned in school and the projects I've worked on there, but Kristof has asked "But how does that relate to your liiiiiife?" about twenty times.

I want to scream. *I'm a single mom with four-year-old twins. My life is Disney, Legos, and what's on the back of this week's cereal box.* But, I'm already painfully aware of how much I do not fit in here; I don't think highlighting that I got pregnant as a teenager is going to help that.

"Okay…" Kristof starts, getting up to walk over to the windowsill where he picks up a baseball and begins to toss it up and catch it. "So, where do you see yourself in five years?"

My mind goes completely blank. Absolutely nothing registers as an answer for a full ten seconds. I realize I opened my mouth to speak, and I quickly close it since there are no words even close to forming complete sentences here.

All of a sudden, Elliott pops into my head, and then Phoebe and Louisa. I don't know why, but I never put the three of them together in my imagination before. It feels familiar though, somehow, like a favorite blanket from childhood—broken in and frayed at the edges from loving use. The image of them together just fits.

That's what I want in five years. It's what I want right now and ten years from now and another ten from that.

God, I really screwed things up.

"Zoey?" Kristof interrupts my mental divergence.

"Sorry. I hadn't really thought about that question before." Kristof frowns. *Crap, wrong answer.* "I mean…" I scramble with a quick smile. "I've been really focused on finishing up school. I've been thinking in more of a one or two year time frame."

Kristof nods, but I can tell I've already added yet another strike against me. "Okay, so what do the next couple years look like?"

I bullshit my way through an answer to the question and we continue to stumble through our awkward interview.

"Well, those are all my questions for you," Kristof says with what looks like relief. Maybe I'm imagining it, but I get the feeling this interview hasn't been a bag of fun for either party. "Do you have any questions for me?"

"Sure. What's work/life balance look like here?" I know I will take just about any job I get offered—that whole beggars-and-choosers business—but this is hands down my biggest worry about a corporate job. When the hours aren't clearly defined, what are the real hours?

"Yeah, good question." I've known Kristof for less than an hour, but I can already tell he's lying through his teeth. He must think my question matches my pinstripe outfit—outdated and cliché. "We have a lot of fun here. We're a really close-knit company. Every team is like a family. So, it really helps with the long hours. We have a lot of work, which is great for an agency. We're super relevant in our industry. We all push really hard, but it's together, you know? So, it feels balanced."

Strike. Strike. Strike. STRIKE.

I somehow make it through my mental list of questions without dashing out of his office, though everything about this place is so not a good fit and I really just want to bail.

We make it to the final handshake, and Kristof lets me know they'll be in touch.

I know it won't be with a job offer, and even though that's kind of depressing, I'm really grateful. I would be miserable, and if one thing's for sure, that's not where I want to be in five years.

Chapter 50

Elliott

I'm lying in the middle of a half-constructed particle board desk at our new office, spinning a hex wrench into oblivion when Brandon walks over. "Yes?" I ask without bothering to look up.

"After you're done with those ten pages of stick-man-instruction hell, can we whiteboard some of the product details we talked about last week? I really want to be fresh when I speak with our advisers tomorrow."

"Sure." I mean for it to come out as a simple one-word response, but the tone of my voice is low and gravelly. I sound more like a teenager than a cofounder of a new company.

Brandon's been patient with me, but even he has his limits. I can tell I'm reaching them before he even opens his mouth to respond. "Dude, you've been sulking all week. Every time I see you, you've got this look on your face like something crawled up your butt and decided to camp out for a while."

"I'm fine." It comes out as a snap, and I follow it up with a deep inhale. It isn't Brandon's fault I'm worse than a pimply fifteen-year-old in braces.

"I know you're fine, but you're kind of a killjoy. No one wants to be around you."

I shoot him a death stare, but apparently my laser blasters aren't on because Brandon doesn't look the least bit fazed.

He starts to walk away from his little pep talk, but he stops and turns around. He shifts from one foot to the other and stuffs his hands into his pockets like he's debating whether or not to push it. "Just answer me this. Do you want to be with her?"

I sit up and lean against my knees, my shoulders dipped in defeat. I've thought this through a million times and kicked myself at the end of every single mental repeat. "Of course I do, but I screwed up. She pushed, and I walked. I did exactly what she was so worried about."

"Then go prove that you're going to show up, and keep showing up."

I shake my head. "It's not that simple."

"Yes it is, dude. Trust isn't some magical thing that shows up overnight while you're sleeping. I know about single moms. She's not going to trust you all at once. It's going to take time and effort, but if you really want to be with her, then it's worth it."

I don't know what to say. It feels about as impossible as making it to the end of this do-it-yourself desk project without having to drill extra holes because the originals don't line up. Fortunately, Brandon seems content to drop the subject and he walks away, letting me stew on it by myself.

I try to get back to focusing on the step-by-step of this desk, but my brain is not cooperating. I walked away from Zoey because she started pushing the stepdad-readiness test. I'm not ready, but Brandon's train of thought sort of applies. I'm not going to wake up ready to be a stepdad any more than Zoey is going to wake up with unwavering trust in me. You have to dive in and hope to god you can keep treading water.

Chapter 51

Zoey

"I love you like you're breakfast," I sing along loudly while I drive Sir Chugs to the airport to drop Cassie off. My pitch is stumbling and way off center, clashing with the sweetly auto-tuned voice on the radio, but I'll do anything to avoid saying goodbye to Cassie. Hell, even thinking about it is off limits.

We must be on the same page because she's singing along too, although clearly, one of us is destined for stardom. Cassie looks and sounds like she's in the middle of a music video. I look more like a wildly delusional fan who makes hundreds of videos on YouTube that get a grand total of ten views.

The song ends and Cassie looks over at me with a smirk. "You know she was saying 'I love you like I'm reckless,' right?"

I squint in concentration, mentally repeating the chorus that had probably been repeated fifty times in the course of three minutes. *Thank you Top 40 cookie cutter machine. This is going to be in my head for the next two weeks.*

Yeah, it was definitely something about breakfast. I shake my head at Cassie. She thumbs her phone open and in five seconds, we're listening to the song again. She holds it up to my ear, just to make sure I'm listening.

"Okay, fine." I can see how it could be reckless. I guess the song has a more emo vibe than lighthearted whimsy. Whatever.

Cassie pulls her phone away smugly and laughs. "Breakfast… You're crazy."

I am irrationally drawn to validating my misinterpretation. "Hey, breakfast is amazing. Loving you more than breakfast would be a big deal. I mean, come on. Bacon."

"I love you, but you're batshit."

"Come on! Bacon? And not that microwaveable, precooked crap. The good stuff, fresh out of the oven." I'm serious now. I can't cook for anything, but it doesn't mean I can't appreciate a good breakfast spread.

"Okay, I can see the drool from over here. I still think you're crazy."

"Fine, I call dibs on all your bacon from here on out. You obviously don't love it enough to be worthy of its deliciousness." I smile as I tease her. *Man, I'm going to miss Cassie.*

I pull up to the bank of sliding doors at the airport departures wing, and I already feel the ball in my throat starting to grow heavy. I'm not ready for Cassie to leave, but classes start in another week. She needs to get back to her life out there. Even though it isn't permanent, I feel like I'm losing my best friend at the exact moment I need her most.

I pull over and park crookedly next to the curb. I know I'm taking up two lanes of space, but I don't want to waste a second fixing it. I have that feeling lurching up from my stomach like I'm about to miss my bus. I have five million things I want to say, and now I only have two minutes to say them.

I step out of the car and meet Cassie up on the sidewalk.

"I'm going to miss you." It's hard for me to even get the words out, but I feel like I might explode if I try to hold them in.

"I'll be home for Christmas. That'll be here in two seconds and a vodka shot." She smiles, but I can see her eyes turning down at the corners just like mine.

"I know."

"And we have these fancy things called phones. I'll buy a bottle of wine. You buy a bottle of wine. We can sit and video chat and drink together." I imagine us, old and wrinkly, sitting on our respective porches at each end of the country with our wine bottles and smartphones. All the feels. All of them.

"You'll be too busy doing the will-we, won't-we dance with Mr. Instructor," I joke.

Cassie purses her lips and brushes me off with a wave of her hand. I know it's been at the back of her mind all summer. She hasn't mentioned it more than once or twice, but she also didn't say yes to any of the guys who showed interest in her over the past couple months. You don't work as a waitress with an amazing personality and legs that could headline a Victoria Secret catwalk without getting more than a few numbers scribbled on napkins.

"Just try to be a little less stupid than me, okay?" I ask. I still feel like a complete screw-up over everything that happened with

Elliott.

Cassie pulls me in for a hug and then smacks my butt with a cheeky grin as she pulls away. "You're not stupid. You're just a fool in love. Besides, you already know what I think you should do."

We've spent more than a few nights talking about it. I still can't figure out how I actually go about fixing the situation. "It's just not that easy," I counter.

"Zoey, love isn't easy. That doesn't mean it isn't worth the effort."

I give her another hug and when we pull away, I see her eyes are starting to get wet.

"I need to check in before the only seats left are the poop deck rows in the back. It's a morning flight. Everyone's going to be drinking coffee and using those bathrooms. There's not enough air freshener in the world to stop that smell from ruining at least a five row radius."

"Fine, go get a decent seat. Call me when you're home, OK?"

"Okay, Mom," Zoey chides, grabbing the handle of her suitcase and walking toward the doors. She turns around and mouths, "I love you." *I love you too, Cassie Porter. I love you too.*

I walk back to my car and notice a familiar blond head of hair closing the hatch of the car in front of me. *Shit.* I try to slink by, but my bright pink shirt is practically a neon blinking light saying, *Hey, look at me.*

Nathan turns around and jumps. "Whoa, Zoey. I didn't see you there when I pulled up."

"Yup, just dropping off my sister." *And maybe the face of the Earth while I'm at it.*

"My friend was just dropping me off." He shifts awkwardly from foot to foot.

We're at an airport departure gate, that's kind of the point. "Well, I need to get home." *You know, to the kids who share half your DNA.*

Nathan scrunches his eyebrows together like he's trying to decide how to proceed. I give him a second, and he finally takes a deep breath. "Yeah, so I've been meaning to call you…I got a job out in Colorado. I'm not really going to be back for much other than holidays. I'm… um…not going to get involved…you know, with your daughters."

I don't know whether to kick him in the shins or pump my fists in the air—probably both. I guess I was right. Getting involved sounds nice in theory, but when real life comes a knocking, it doesn't sound so nice after all. Well, I'm glad I stood my ground. He really is a turd—at least now he's a turd I don't have to deal with. "Okay, Nathan. Thanks for letting me know."

He nods and says goodbye, looking a little lighter after running into me. I wish I could say the same, but judging by the ten-pound kettle bell that just dropped to the pit of my stomach, I'm pretty sure I got the short end of this encounter stick.

Chapter 52

Zoey

I'm in the middle of batch number two of chocolate chip cookies when I get a call from Draper and Young letting me know they won't be continuing with my application. Hey, at least they didn't break up with me via Post-It note. They get serious points for calling. When I ask for feedback like all the online job interview advice tells me to, the man from HR tells me they "didn't really get a sense of my personality, so they couldn't confirm that it would be a good cultural fit."

It's the most PC way I've ever been told I wasn't cool enough. From the moment I walked through the front door of the Draper and Young office, it was clear that was going to be the case.

It's a bittersweet relief. I want a job, but I absolutely do not want that job.

While I'm on the phone, my computer chimes with an email alert. I finish the call and click over to see an unfamiliar name with the subject *Announcing This Year's Contest Winner.* My heart flutters, and then drops. They would have contacted me beforehand if I had won.

When I open it, I scan down to see that some guy named Chad won the internship. Suddenly, it doesn't feel so good to have bombed at Draper and Young. I need a job more than I need work/life balance.

My phone strums with a text, and I almost want to hide it under the couch cushion. I'm done with bad news for today, but I'm pretty sure none of the jobs I've applied for would text me. So, I turn it over. Elliott.

I'd really like to talk.

Are you free today?

My heart quickens with excitement. I was going to message him as soon as I finished these cookies, but he beat me to it. Running into Nathan yesterday startled me into action. Staring directly at the shit hand life originally dealt me made me appreciate the ace I was handed in this past round.

I finally realized it doesn't matter how I fix it. It only matters that I show Elliott I'm willing to try—emphasis on the trying part, since batch one of my great cookie bribery plan ended in a charred mess.

I know without a doubt I don't want to be a single parent. It may protect my daughters, but preventing us from ever being hurt isn't going to make any of us better people. I was acting out of fear with a healthy dose of mama bear thrown in. Yes, Elliott walked away, but I pushed him.

I punch in my reply.

Yes. 6pm?

His response strums almost immediately.

Great. Let's meet at the park.

I sneak out just before dinner with a quick excuse about running an errand. None of the other three females in the house bat an eye, so either I'm a really good liar, or entirely expendable.

Probably both.

Either way, I'm anxious as hell, and I practically sprint to the park. My nerves temporarily short-circuit the pain receptors, but I regret the choice as soon as I stop. My legs are on fire and the summer heat kicked my sweat production into high gear—not to mention, I forgot I was carrying a bag of cookies in my backpack. Whoops.

I'm a thoroughly winded, completely out of shape, drenched mess—not exactly the look I was going for when meeting the man I completely screwed things up with last week. I debate running back home, but I both doubt my legs will carry me that far and don't want to risk Elliott thinking I'm standing him up.

I see his red car pull up just as I make it to the bench. I watch him step out, and everything fades away to one single thought.

I have to fix this.

Then, I notice he's carrying a plate with him. He takes a few steps and I swear I smell bacon. I look again at the plate and see that my nose was spot on. He made me pancakes and bacon.

It feels like an eternity until he finally reaches the bench. He offers the plate to me with a self-conscious tilt of his head. "I never got to make you breakfast after you stayed over."

My heart feels like it's endlessly skipping on smooth water. "Are you trying to win me over through my stomach, Elliott

MacCallister?"

"Is it working?" He smiles hopefully.

"Maybe." I take a bite of fluffy pancake and moan. *Crap, was that out loud? Oh well, these are delicious.* They deserve a full *When Harry Met Sally* treatment. "Um, switch that to a *yes*."

Elliott rewards me with a laugh and I mentally flog myself for staying away. I love that sound. What was I thinking running away from it?

I pull out the bag of cookies that look like a steaming congealed mess of chocolate mixed in with blobs of dough. "Um, I tried to make you cookies. It didn't really work out so well."

Elliott laughs again and opens the bag to grab a chunk from the top. He doesn't cough or keel over, which I consider a win. I offer him a piece of bacon and he gladly accepts. We both know who's got the cooking chops, and it's not me.

We're both quiet for a minute. It feels so good just to be near him, but I don't know where to start. The last time we were here, I put a river between us, and I don't know how to start building the bridge to cross it.

Elliott turns to me. "Last week really made me think. You were right. I hadn't been thinking about this as a relationship with more than you, and it is. It was a lot to process, and I didn't do that very well on the spot. I don't know what it's like to be a dad, but I do know what it's like to be a father figure. I'm the closest thing to a dad Stewart has, and being his uncle has easily become one of my favorite things in the world. I know that doesn't automatically qualify me for stepdad material. There's a lot between here and there, but I know you and I are worth the effort. I'm willing to take it slow to prove to you that you can trust me. I'm in love with you, Zoey Porter. I want to be with you, no matter how long it takes or what it looks like."

My heart feels like it's pushing against the constraints of my skin, and I wonder if I might explode into a million pieces from the brutally wonderful force.

"I love you too, Elliott. More than bacon," I add with a cheeky grin. My tone is light but the meaning is heavy. I climb into his lap and thread my fingers through his hair. I want to entangle myself in him completely and permanently.

He reaches out and does the same while he presses his lips to my forehead. "Good, because I don't want to have to compete with the most delicious meat on the planet. It's just not fair."

"Don't worry, you'd win. Besides, you are part of my life now, and I'm going to fight to keep you there." My smile grows wider, and I sink deeper into Elliott's strong arms. I silently wonder if I'll ever be able to stand up again. I feel like a hermit crab that's finally found its permanent shell. It just fits.

"I promise I'll be right there with you every step of the way." Elliott presses his lips to mine and I press every inch of my body to his as we seal our pledge to each other.

We are keeping each other because we finally figured out that when you jump off a cliff, the only thing you can do is reach out for the person next to you and hold on with everything you've got.

Epilogue

Six Months Later

Zoey

My phone starts to buzz, gently rattling my desk. I slip off my massive headphones that cover the entire circumference of my ears and office sounds flood back in.

I quickly silence my alarm—a reminder to pick the girls up from full-day preschool.

I stuff my phone into my messenger bag and drag my mouse over to the upper right corner of my computer so it closes to black.

"See ya, Zoey," my desk neighbor, Steve, says with a smile. We started at Grassroots, a small marketing company, on the same day last September.

After sending my resume around like a mindless Internet bot, I saw a post for openings here. I loved the fact they're all about helping small, local businesses build better brands and connect with their community. I knew immediately I couldn't just be one of the ten thousand applicants. I figured out one of the founders has kids the same age as mine, so I asked around and figured out they go to the same preschool my girls do. It only took two weekends of shameless stalking and one "Hey, you're Sheila Barnett, right?" before I had a job.

Okay, so there was a grueling day of interviews and plenty of I-hope-they-like-me-as-much-as-I-like-them anxiety, but I got it.

When I was freaking out about whether or not I had nailed the interview, Elliott offered me a job on his new team.

I think my exact words were, "I already tried dating my boss's brother. I don't think dating my actual boss is a step in the right direction."

I get in Sir Chugs and make my way toward the old brick school building. We're in the last few weeks of winter, and the heat finally kicks in to warm up the car.

There's already a long line down the block when I arrive. The muffled sounds of laughter and happy shouts stream in, and my heart overflows with pure joy. The girls love their new school. They're always coming home with some sort of craft, and I'm such a sucker for their artwork. I've already stuffed an entire file organizer full for each of them. If I keep it up, there's going to be a whole *Hoarders* episode dedicated to the mother who couldn't even throw away her children's ten-year-old cotton ball lamb construction paper projects, and I'll be the star.

It's finally my turn to pull into the circular drive of the school entrance and the girls skip toward the car, opening the back door and climbing in with overlapping explanations of yet another best day ever. Apparently, they constructed paper mailboxes today in preparation for the Valentine's Day celebration tomorrow.

By the time we get home, I've heard the full play-by-play of the entire day. Who brought what for snack time. What the letter of the day was. The exact lineup of the obstacle course Ms. Myers set up for gym class.

Everything I've worked so hard for in the past five years has led me to these moments. It's so simple, but it's my favorite thing in the world to pick up Phoebe and Louisa and hear about the amazing adventures of their blissfully normal days.

Well, second favorite.

I barely shift the car into park before they unbuckle out of their booster seats and dash out toward the side door of the house.

I'm right behind them as they open the door and blast in like two excited firecrackers.

"Elliott!" they cry out together. They race toward him, wrapping their tiny arms around his waist in a group hug. He beams down at them as he asks them about their day.

This is the best part of my day. Hands down.

I walk over to him, wrap my arms around his shoulders, and give him a sweet kiss on the cheek.

We saw each other as much as we could by ourselves for a few months until I couldn't take it any more. He never complained or pushed. He waited for me to be ready, and finally, I couldn't think of a single reason not to introduce him to the girls.

It went better than I could have ever imagined. They loved

him. The fact that he played Legos with them for two hours straight certainly didn't hurt, and I loved that they loved him.

Elliott has his own apartment now just down the street, but he comes over to my mom's house every day and the four of us have dinner.

He usually spends Sundays over at Samantha's house with her and Stewart. I haven't been brave enough to venture over there yet, but Elliott assures me Samantha's hostility toward me is waning. I figure I'll give it about another five years, and then maybe we can see about a brief encounter. I wonder if I could convince him to hide all the potential weapons in her house before I show up.

In the meantime, it helps that Elliott feeds me all the good insider information. Stewart was seriously bummed I was gone— which was both gratifying and heartbreaking. He had a rough couple weeks until he started preschool, but now he's thriving again. His teachers love him, and so do all the kids. I mean, who wouldn't? It's Stewart we're talking about here.

Plus, Stewart's new afterschool nanny is a stout British grandmother and the two of them get along famously. Samantha still likes to point out that she's off limits to Elliott, which gives me hope that there's a little humor tucked away in there somewhere.

"What's for dinner?" Louisa asks, eyeing the ingredients lined up on the counter. Elliott gets the girls involved with dinner prep any time he cooks, so maybe they won't grow up to be as hopeless in the kitchen as I am.

"Well, since tomorrow's Valentine's Day, I thought we could have a special meal together tonight," Elliott explains.

My mom is over at Bruce's tonight—a regular occurrence these days. She's going to watch the girls tomorrow so Elliott and I can go out on our own. Cassie is still in LA, so more often than not, it's just the four of us.

"Oooh, what is it?" Phoebe's tone rises at the end in excitement.

Elliott smiles down at them like he has the world in his hands. "Well, we're having lasagna first, and then lava cake for dessert."

"Really?" Louisa's eyes are as big as the mixing bowls set out on the counter.

As if they didn't love him enough already, he keeps winning them over time and time again. When he told me about his plan to make a fancy dinner as a special way to bring a group tradition to a holiday known for celebrating romantic love, I absolutely melted.

"You're my most favorite." Phoebe doesn't hold back. Hey, if I cooked like Elliott, I would be everyone's favorite too.

Elliott smiles adoringly at her. "First though, I thought you all might want to open your gifts."

"Gifts!" they both cry out, not even remotely trying to contain their excitement.

Elliott reaches behind a bag of flour on the counter and pulls out two tiny wrapped boxes. The paper is off in nanoseconds.

The girls shriek as they open each of their boxes to find matching bracelets with four tiny little interlocking hearts in the center. Elliott bends down and they each wrap around him in a giant hug.

When they let go, he stands up and pulls me into his arms. "I love all three of you to the ends of the universe and back."

I reach up and press my lips to his.

"That's good because now that you've started cooking for us, we'd go hungry without you. You've brought us wild animals in. We've forgotten how to feed ourselves. Now you're stuck with us," I joke.

"I've always wanted a band of monkeys," Elliott says with a wide grin.

Phoebe starts jumping around singing, "who-who-who, he-he-he, ha-ha-ha," and Louisa chimes in, creating a monkey chorus. Elliott's smile grows even wider and he starts to chase them around, catching each of them and tossing them up in the air. They shout out in delight, "More! More!"

I stand back and watch the family that's blossoming before my eyes. I think to myself, *I don't know how I got here but damn, I'm glad I made it.*

It's the four of us, now and forever, and there's nothing in the world I would trade for this.

The End

Acknowledgements

Pressing publish on my first book has been a long time coming. There is a long list of people who played a part in this process. Thank you to each and every one of you who asked how my writing was going. Your curiosity fueled my drive to make it happen.

A massive thank you to my family, both by blood and by marriage. Thank you, Haighs, for being my wonderfully loud cheering section. Your support means the world to me. Thanks for taking me in with open arms and loving me even when I'm a grumpy, overwhelmed mess.

Mom, thank you for filling my childhood with creativity and love. My life is full of wonderful stories because of you, and I am forever grateful. Dad, thank you for showing me what it means to live with integrity. Your love for our family is the glue we never see but always know is there holding it all together. And Dawn, this one's for you. Thank you for always trying to make me cooler, even though I will forever be a huge nerd.

Oh my goodness, hugs to the wonderful people who helped turn this Scrivener file into a real book. Judy at Write Technique, you helped me see what I was missing, and Caitlin at Editing by C Marie, you polished this baby up big time. I owe you both serious bacon and pancakes. Thank you Wendy at The Passionate Proofreader for catching those last little invisible buggers. Daniela at DCP Designs, thank you for turning my messy brain of ideas into a gorgeous cover. You are amazing. And Amazon, I heart you. Thank you for giving this indie community a global platform.

Becca, thank you for jumping in and being my Edna, even though I'm pretty sure you're the real superhero here. Your enthusiasm and kindness and SAME BRAIN was more than helpful…it was just the smack on the butt I needed to push this out into the world. I'm so glad you messaged me. Here's to all the doughnuts in our future.

Thank you Erin over at Southern Belle Promotions for being such an organized wizard and getting the word out about this book. Thank you to all the book bloggers and bookstagramers for taking the time to read, comment, and post about Only Fools Jump. You all are lovely people. I wish we could all meet up for drinks after work. Let's get on that, OK?

To my little buddy…your consistently good naps made this book possible. Let's keep this good sleep thing going. P.S. - I love you more than bacon AND French fries AND doughnuts. Always.

Matt, I could write a million and a half love stories, and none of them would be as good as the one I have with you. Thank you for being the best husband and father in the whole universe. This book exists because you propped me up while I worked my butt off. Sorry that I frequently forgot to shower or make dinner. Thank you for loving me anyway.

And finally, dear reader, thank you for taking a chance on a new indie author. Every time you click purchase or post a picture or write a review, you're giving us a virtual fist bump. That may not seem like a lot, but every click, every like fuels more words and more stories. We keep writing because you keep showing up.

Until next time...

XO,
K.P.

About K.P. Haigh

K.P. Haigh joined the adult world as a project manager. After spending years in spreadsheets, she put her love of blank notebooks to good use and started spinning words into love stories.

In a perfect world, K.P. would have a never-ending supply of coffee, carbs, and sticky notes. She corners the market on ridiculous facial expressions and is happiest when she's cooking for people or making them laugh.

She's always up for crispy French fries and can't wait for self-driving cars to take over the world so she can read on her way to everywhere.

K.P. lives in Seattle with the man who loves her crazy and their son, who inherited half of it.

Follow K.P. Haigh

Newsletter: kphaigh.com/newsletter
Instagram: instagram.com/kphaigh
Facebook: facebook.com/kphaigh
Website: kphaigh.com

Mr. Sportsball by K.P. Haigh
Releasing Fall 2016

Montgomery Bell craves adventure—the kind that knocks on your door and drags you out by your half-slept-on hair because it can't wait another second.

The problem is, she still lives thirty minutes from her hometown, and it's known for one thing: football. Montgomery wouldn't know the difference between an interception and a fumble if one hit her in the face.

When she meets Baron Richards, it practically does.

Baron is a rising star in the professional football world. Their worlds collide, sending Montgomery on the kind of adventure she never even thought to look for.

Finding love isn't the end of the story. You have to figure out what to do with it once you catch it, and run like hell to make that happen.

Don't worry, Montgomery's running...she just doesn't quite know which direction yet.

Mr. Sportsball *is not your typical sports romance. It's a full-length, standalone novel that will have fans and anti-fans cheering for the same team.*

www.ingramcontent.com/pod-product-compliance
Lightning Source LLC
Chambersburg PA
CBHW020247180626
46810CB00006B/2406